CW01506913

ADVANCE PRAI

"Thrilling and brilliantly crafted, *Mr. Gobscheit* plunges readers into a high-stakes world of espionage, blending wit, intrigue, and timely geopolitical themes in a page-turning classic for anyone interested at all in what's coming for Ireland and the western world!"
– LP O'Bryan, award-winning author of The Istanbul Puzzle.

"*Mr Gobscheit* is a brilliantly told thriller, filled with intrigue and double dealing. Many characters bear a striking resemblance to personalities we all seem to know. Center stage is Ireland and its adjacent undersea communication cables, critical to NATO and under threat by Russian antagonists. I really enjoyed this book."
– L. Michael Hager is cofounder and former Director General, International Development Law Organization, Rome.

"*Mr. Gobscheit* is a gripping, high-stakes thriller that masterfully captures the complexity of modern alliances and the relentless courage required to safeguard them. Mark Jamison's journey—from the depths of undersea intrigue to the corridors of political power—is a powerful reminder of the delicate balance upon which global security rests. With a storyline that feels both timely and urgent, this novel immerses readers in a world of danger, loyalty, and sacrifice. A must-read for anyone who loves a tale of resilience and action grounded in real-world stakes."
– Captain Brett Crozier, United States Navy (Ret.)

MR. GOBSCHEIT
(IT'S ALL GOBSCHEIT)

AVERY MANN

A MARK JAMISON THRILLER

TROWBRIDGEARCHER
PUBLISHERS

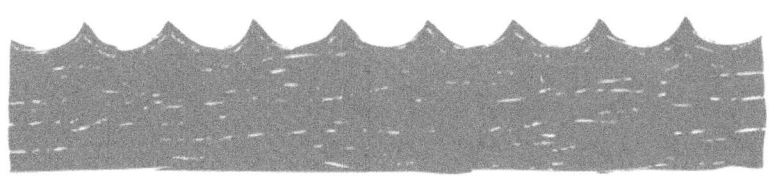

TrowbridgeArcher Publishers
653 Barcelona Drive
Sonoma, California 95476-4436

TROWBRIDGEARCHER
PUBLISHERS

ISBN: **979-8-9884045-9-0**

CHAPTER

1

Foggy Gorgarty

It was a crisp morning. Yellow streaks broke through the white-fringed gray clouds lazing above their love nest on the hillside in Angel Landing. Mark Jamison was enjoying watching Sarah fall back into slumber after a morning's romancing, shared with the abandon of knowing their children were now grown and living far away.

It was time to get up and prepare coffee and present it dutifully to Sarah on her first glimpse of daylight. But then the phone rang unexpectedly, with Bjorn Ingman providing the briefest of cryptic messages.

"Sorry to ring so early, Mark. But you are about to receive an important call, so time to stir. I'll see you for lunch with the trolls later at the club." Before Mark could ask anything at all, Bjorn hung up.

It was only a moment or two before the phone rang again. At first, he thought he was getting a weather report.

"Mark, it's Foggy!"

"I'm sorry. Who is this, please?"

"Oh, come on, Jamison, how many Foggys could you possibly know?"

"There is only one Mr. Gorgarty in my address book. And sure and that's quite enough now!" Jamison responded with his best attempt at a Gaelic brogue for this time of the morning.

"To what in the world do I owe this honor? Foggy, I've missed you, but you seem to have disappeared for the last few years. It's really great to hear your voice."

"Well, get dressed and get down the hill for coffee with me at Café Acre. You can hear lots more of my enchanting voice and even see the results of too much good eating over the last years."

"Foggy, you mean you're here at Angel Landing?"

"Yes, and waiting for you for my second cup. Hurry now. And don't bother to shave. I didn't this morning. Actually haven't for the last year or so. Blow a kiss to your lovely bride and step lively. Lots of catching up."

With that, Foggy hung up.

As he threw on some clothes and headed out the door, Jamison searched his memories of the charming Irishman.

He never thought he would meet anyone with the name "Foggy." Jamison had worked at Foggy Bottom, what had grown to be an affectionate name for the US State Department in Washington, DC. And many who worked there were known for the mushy reports that never satisfied the certainty that was so elusive in government relations. But Foggy? That individual was introduced at a consular reception in Hong Kong a very long time ago.

Jamison could still recall Foggy's voice, his stunning eyes, and the explanation for his unusual name.

"My parents were part of the Gorgarty clan, well known in Dublin and to many pubgoers there. But my mother's family was Fogarty. So they christened me with the melodic, or at least rhyming name, Fogarty Gorgarty, Foggy to my friends. You are now among those, Mark." Jamison was delighted by the honor and Foggy would indeed grow to be a friend.

The relationship that evening in Hong Kong involved a number of commonalities. Foggy was a serving officer in the Royal Navy at the time, and Mark had recently wound up his active service and retained his reserve naval commission, while he transitioned to diplomatic work at State.

Jamison's assignment to Hong Kong was to represent the USA, which was being sued by a Tokyo-based shipping company for the loss of several boats that had been chartered at the end of the Vietnam War. The boats were used to carry cargoes and personnel across the Tonle Sap and down the Mekong. The boats were a sensitive subject because, as Mark discovered in the vaults of the Defense Intelligence Agency, they were bringing gold, drugs, and undercover personnel out of Cambodia. When Vietnam fell, the boats were taken over by communist forces. Mark's legal defense was that the bareboat charters had terminated and the boats reverted to their Japanese corporate owner.

Arriving in Hong Kong, Jamison was informed that what was then known as the Canton Trade Fair was in full progress and that no accommodation would be found anywhere in Hong Kong or Kowloon. He decided to push on to see Ginny Carson at the consulate, who suggested the evening's cocktail reception. There, the charming and loquacious young British officer gained his attention and, after several champagnes, offered his stateroom in the harbor for Mark's temporary accommodation. This was Foggy. After a night aboard his ship, Foggy arranged a room for Mark ashore at the posh Royal Navy officers club. And when Mark wasn't engaged with his case, Foggy hosted him around to Repulse Bay, to gambling at Macao and to horse racing at Sha Tin. Foggy seemed to allow his inner Irishman to blossom forth in Mark's company. That was something frowned upon by his Royal Navy shipmates.

Over time, they kept in touch, but Foggy had literally fallen off Mark's radar for at least the last four or five years. It would be a treat to learn what this enjoyable old friend was up to. But why such a rushed meeting after all this time? Mark could sure use the coffee to help with his bafflement.

**

On entering the café, Foggy stood and waved Mark to his table, offering a salute, bear hug, and ludicrously overdone kiss on both cheeks before allowing him to sit. Foggy's shock of curly red hair was still evident, but some gray was now creeping into his trim beard. Considerably shorter than Jamison's six feet two inches, Foggy was built stockier and maintained a more muscular, athletic appearance. But those unmistakable eyes! One was blue and the other hazel green. All in all, he looked in top form.

After the usual pleasantries were concluded, Foggy confessed to being on an official task and that he had only a short while before he was being picked up and on his way back to the San Francisco Airport. He apologized for needing to cut to the chase and offered that their next meeting would provide more of an opportunity to catch up. Mark was silent and worked his way through two cups of French roast while Gorgarty proceeded to explain that he was now working ostensibly for the Garda Síochána, on the intelligence side, and reporting also to the Military Intelligence Corps of the Irish Defense Forces.

"We are responsible for gathering and analyzing information related to potential threats to Ireland's security. But off the record, I am also on a confidential assignment from NATO Headquarters in Brussels, which is why I'm here."

Through Foggy's presentation, Jamison learned that he was still talked about for his role years earlier in persuading Hungary to join NATO. Foggy said he had been sent to request Mark to take on a new assignment that would have them working together in Ireland.

"Listen, Mark," Gorgarty explained, "Russia is having frequent naval exercises on the edges of Irish-controlled waters. You know something about the sabotage of the Nord Stream gas pipelines in the Baltic Sea. Well, the situation that's unfolding puts the security of transatlantic cables front and center in Ireland and NATO. We know that about three-quarters of all cables in the northern hemisphere pass through or near Irish waters, most off the southwest coast and some off the northwest coast. These cables carry 97 percent of global communications, including financial transactions, business operations, and everyday internet access. We think that supporters of Irish neutrality have to give way when it comes to protecting the life support of us all, including you Yanks.

"Now comes the ask. Our meeting today was cleared by your old bosses who want you back. You would be joining me in Dublin for a cover assignment. The stakes are very high because the threats are increasing with the tensions over Ukraine and now Iran. If the cables go, it won't matter about the satellites. Now that everyone knows satellite-relayed traffic is monitored, the real stuff goes encrypted through undersea fiber-optic cables. But you know all about that, I'm sure.

"I know your kids are grown enough to be out of the house. We could find preschool teaching for Sarah in Dublin. She and my wife would get on famously."

Jamison sat somewhat astonished, but very pleased to be remembered at all after so many years. He responded cautiously.

"Foggy, there must be others who could handle this. I would really enjoy working with you, but we are happily ensconced here and frankly, Sarah's been through enough with my assignments... even with things that have gone on here. But I think there is something more to this, something you aren't telling me."

"Right as usual, Jamison. Really, two things. First, my new assignment is with the deputy defense minister, whose office has picked up responsibility for telecommunications security. That includes undersea cable security, which is where you and I fit into the picture."

"OK." Jamison pushed Foggy to his second point. "What's the other thing?"

"Well, between us"—Foggy looked around the café to be sure they were quite alone in their area—"this chap may be working for the Russians. Either that or he's a complete imbecile."

"What's his name?"

"Gobscheit."

"That's a name? What else?"

"Frankly, I was told to expect your answer, but I think this request is nonnegotiable."

Gorgarty's car pulled up and he left with a parting hug and admonition to Jamison about thinking it over and getting his affairs in order quickly.

***

The following week, a receipted overnight letter arrived addressed to Captain Mark Jamison, USN. He immediately noticed the word "retired" or "RET" was missing. Opening it, he found orders recalling him to active duty with his reserve rank of naval captain. He was to report in forty-eight hours to the Office of Naval Intelligence (ONI) in Suitland, Maryland. It is America's oldest intelligence-gathering organization, established in 1882.

To Sarah's puzzlement, he explained that the receipt of retired pay meant being subject to recall at the needs of the service. There was no choice offered. But Mark assured her to carry on as normal here at Angel Landing until he could pin things down further. There was no need for her to be alarmed. He had some calls to make and some research to do to check out the basics of what Foggy was conveying.

CHAPTER

2

Homework

By chance, the Jamisons had visited Valentia Island on a journey to Ireland some years earlier. They intended to take the ferry to County Kerry's celebrated Dingle Peninsula, but the wet and cold brisk winds off the Atlantic didn't permit. So they contented themselves with explorations on the most westwardly point of the Iveragh Peninsula. Valentia Island is home to Knights Town, known for the first telegraphic cable landing station connecting North America to Europe. Ireland played a central role then and continues to do so.

    The Atlantic Telegraph Company was formed in 1856, with the ambitious goal of laying a telegraph cable across the Atlantic Ocean. This would revolutionize communication between Europe and North America, reducing the time it took to send messages from weeks to mere hours. Sailing ships outfitted with miles of cable left Newfoundland and Knights Town to rendezvous and link up in mid ocean. Attempts in 1857 and 1858 were unsuccessful, but the third attempt in 1865 was a resounding success, remaining in service for over twenty years.

In the early twentieth century, coaxial cables were developed, offering higher capacity and improved signal quality compared to earlier technologies.

The invention of optical fiber cables in the 1960s revolutionized telecommunications. As global trade, business, and communication expanded, the demand for transatlantic cables grew. Ireland's geographic position on the western edge of Europe made it a strategic location for cable landings. Ireland's robust infrastructure and connectivity also made it a significant data hub, attracting businesses and data centers, including Apple Computer's new European headquarters. To say Ireland was a vital hub for transatlantic communications was really an understatement. The island was one large switching platform essential to modern data integration, including that of finance, commerce, industry, and defense... NATO writ large.

Jamison's inquiries turned up the AE6 cable, the major transatlantic route connecting Ireland to the United States, the TGN-Atlantic cable system, and Seacom, primarily focused on connecting Africa to Europe, and also linked through Ireland to the rest of the world. It seemed Ireland was investing heavily in its offshore infrastructure, such as subsea cables, gas pipelines and the Celtic

Interconnector, and an underwater electricity link between Cork and Brittany that would have the capacity to power 450,000 homes.

Neutral Ireland has been a partner with NATO since 1999, when it joined the Partnership for Peace program. That was set up to strengthen security relationships between NATO and non-member countries. Ireland then joined a new agreement with NATO to protect against potential threats to undersea infrastructure and cybersecurity. This was the Individually Tailored Partnership Programme (ITPP), which allows for greater information and intelligence sharing. The agreement resulted from an increased hybrid threat level due to the war in Ukraine.

Jamison also reviewed the Pacific undersea cable system, which has far less redundancy. All Asian traffic, even that beamed through microwave towers, coalesces into a series of networks under the South China Sea that feed into one central fiber-optic cable that emerges six feet under a beach near Morro Bay, California. The information contained in that cable is fed through AT&T lines to a station near San Luis Obispo, then heads directly to 611 Folsom Street in San Francisco. Eighty percent of all Asian traffic enters the US in this fashion, crossing the Pacific in five-hundredths of a second, at the speed of light. At Folsom Street, the traffic heads to the seventh floor, where it is joined with domestic traffic. As impossible as it seems, the totality of everything, telecommunications, financial transactions, commercial and personal internet messages, then heads down one floor to a top-secret space operated by AT&T in conjunction with the US National Security Agency (NSA). Here, since 2003, all traffic then passes through a fiber-optic splitter, with a duplicate of everything going directly to the NSA at Suitland, Maryland.

There are between fifteen and thirty similar facilities located across the US. Traffic from Africa and the Middle East gets routed through Europe, then to stations in Ireland before crossing the Atlantic and being processed by the NSA at Augusta, Georgia.

All in all, 99 percent of all internet traffic goes on 493 active subsea internet cables. That's well over a million miles of undersea data wires. Copper conductors are used to boost the signals every fifty miles or so. Today, dense wave division multiplexing is used with several wavelengths stacked at landing sites. One fiber-optic wire sends, one receives, all bundled in a single cable. Jamison reread the reports: "An estimated 99 percent of intercontinental internet traffic and data and voice communication passes through fiber-optic submarine cables along the ocean floor, facilitating over $10 trillion worth of financial transactions daily. These carry sensitive government communications, including overseas military operations."

There was one more item that Jamison discovered. In 2013, Edward Snowden revealed the

NSA taps certain cables to monitor all communications that pass through them, even those never bound for the USA.

CHAPTER

3

The Assignment

Mark Jamison reported on schedule to ONI, now part of the National Maritime Intelligence Center, located on the grounds of the Suitland Federal Center in Suitland, Maryland.

Things there grew greatly more complex since his career days. ONI was still led by a commander, formally known as the Commander, Office of Naval Intelligence, but she now also served as Director of the National Maritime Intelligence-Integration Office, the national intelligence community's center for maritime issues. Her functions included fulfilling all national maritime intelligence duties through a number of separate centers, including those charged with data transmission through undersea cables.

All the usual data entry formalities of returning to active service occupied most of the morning. A phone call earlier relieved him of the need to pack a uniform, and he was feeling pretty chipper about the entire matter. The ordeal of administrative paperwork included reaffirmations associated with his continuing security clearances. When through with it all, Mark was escorted by a lieutenant through the sprawling complex for Jamison's meeting with the ONI director.

On the way, they passed the Farragut Technical Analysis Center for strategic scientific and technical intelligence analysis. The lieutenant said he understood that some of Captain Jamison's briefings would take place there. He said the center housed the National Maritime Acoustic Intelligence Laboratory.

The lieutenant also pointed out the Hopper Center, which supports global maritime and intelligence operations. Its staff consists of more than 850 information technology specialists based in 42 locations in 11 countries. The center also assists in the integration, testing, fielding, and maintenance of advanced technologies utilized by ONI and its centers.

They then came to the ONI director's suite of offices. Jamison was invited to sit down across from her imposing and clutter-free mahogany desk, while the lieutenant was excused and left, closing the door behind him.

The rear admiral directing ONI showed her awareness that then Hungarian president Ferenc Mádl gave Mark full credit for raising and encouraging the possibility of Hungary joining NATO and moving the process along. She also knew of Mark's efforts to see it through with contacts at State, the White House, and at Brussels.

To the question "Do you know why you are here?", Mark paused and said simply that he follows orders.

"What would you think about persuading Ireland to join NATO, working circumspectly, of course? You would need to find out who is on board and who is working against the idea. This role seems perfectly suited to someone with your skill set, and, frankly, Brussels asked for you specifically."

"Thank you for your confidence in me. As I said, I follow orders and am under orders here right now. But I must say, I think a lot of Irish neutrality and have been pleased with the independence of Ireland's foreign policy. I met Mary Robinson before she became Ireland's first woman president. She was then head of the humanitarian activities of the United Nations and I was most impressed with her and with standing up for human rights around the world."

"Would it matter to you if Ireland's undersea cables were threatened by Russia? What if we have intelligence that Russia wants to break up NATO's ability to resist an expanding Ukrainian war that could be heading into Poland? Or that our Congress might require NATO membership before we could come to the aid of Ireland? We set up a Space Force to deal with satellite security. Brussels wants to set up a kind of seabed security force. The fiber-optic cables account for vastly more traffic than satellites. What if both were cut off?"

"Yes, Admiral, these are certainly interesting possibilities and issues. But Ireland is only a short distance from the UK and British units could come to the aid of Ireland quickly and easily, with or without NATO."

"Mark, have you thought about the history of these countries? Do you suppose that having the British in Ireland may be a problem?"

"Well, I will leave the decisions with the decision makers but will try my best to give an accurate picture to the proper authorities in Ireland and at NATO."

"Excuse me, Captain Jamison. But who do you suppose you'll be working for?"

"Yes, of course. I am to report to you, I take it?"

"That would be the appropriate answer for an officer under orders to this command. You will be in contact with our staff at the embassy in Dublin. Do you know Captain Tom Harrington, our naval attaché there? I'm sure you will both get on very well.

"Please get to know our staff over the next few days. You will also have briefings from our NATO folks here. We will be working up your cover assignment as a liaison in the Irish Defense Ministry. You know Foggy Gorgarty already. He is fully clued in and has asked for you. He's on our side, at least as far as we can tell. After finishing up here in a week or so, feel free to head back to Angel

Landing with pay and benefits for a month's leave prior to reporting to Captain Harrington."

"Who will I be reporting to in the Irish ministry?"

"Gobscheit."

"Is that a name?"

"Good afternoon, Captain. I look forward to running into you at some of your briefings. I'm off to the Pentagon for the rest of today and tomorrow. The Middle East and Ukraine are not quieting down as we hoped, and China is China."

As Mark stood to leave, with her door still closed, the director said one more thing.

"We know you are aware of how Nord Stream 2 charges were prepositioned and detonated. What if I told you that we have radiation monitoring consistent with at least one small yield nuclear device attached to Ireland's AE6 cable? That information doesn't leave this room. But as you consider the seriousness of your assignment, realize that a detonation there would not only sever all communication that passes through it, but would release an electromagnetic pulse that would fry the sending and receiving stations, as well as possibly interrupting all communication on the seabed. What I am saying to you, Captain, is that would cut off the States from the rest of NATO and effectively leave the organization paralyzed."

CHAPTER

4

Tom Harrington

Back at Angel Landing, the Jamisons were explaining that the American political mess and gun violence were causing them to relocate to a calmer and safer place. It wasn't far from the truth, just not all of it. Some friends wanted to join their emigration. Many invitations and farewells were accompanied by the rejoinder of "Please come visit us." But secretly, Mark and Sarah were ready for a new adventure and saw Angel Landing growing a bit small and confining. Even Bjorn Ingman and the troll lunches at the yacht club offered friendship but not the excitement of gale-force wind in the face they recalled from their earlier sojourn with the kids to Valentia Island. Adam and Adrienne were delighted their folks were heading to Ireland and looked forward to visits to the pubs they were too young to fully appreciate before.

Jamison made good use of the month being in touch with phone calls to Foggy and to Captain Tom Harrington. Harrington was enjoying a payback posting to Dublin as naval attaché, after a distinguished career that included overseeing some off-the-record SEALS and Delta Force operations in Afghanistan, Iraq, and Northern Jordan. Through long and dangerous deployments, Tom's wife had enough and left him, taking their four kids. He was apparently now making the best of it on the bachelor scene as a suave American diplomat in Ireland.

When Jamison called to talk about his job and housing, Harrington would shine him along, saying his aide was looking into suitable housing and that Foggy would be briefing him on his cover when he arrived. Of course, since they were speaking on unsecure phone lines, Jamison could really not expect much more. Harrington always shifted the conversation back to his new passion and hoped that Jamison would share it when he arrived.

"The English were damn fools to outlaw fox hunting in 2004," Harrington explained. "Now the Irish are poking their thumbs into the Brits' eyes by expanding the popularity of the sport."

Harrington belonged to a riding club organized by Seamus McGrath and rode to the hounds at Newtown Garristown in County Dublin.

Political correctness in Ireland, it seemed, extended to humane policies toward the treatment of human beings around the world. In this regard, the Irish stayed clear to the extent possible from a British foreign policy aggressively aligned with

American global hegemony. But the Brits wanted to show their humanness toward the little wild creatures as a sort of snubbing their own royals favorite pastime. Now the Irish could take their comeuppance and take over all the pomp and ceremony, not to mention the sheer excitement of the fox hunts.

Seamus told Tom that he was born to hunt but forced to work. Harrington described the McGrath home as one he always wanted for himself, filled with leather boots and riding paraphernalia. And of course, a German Pointer named Otto who presided over all and kept in line McGrath's race horses, Jerry, Shadow, and Molly. Harrington described the allure of their wearing green coats with yellow collars, and hunting stock white cravats over white shirts and white britches. He was proud to say that McGrath occasionally let him sound the bugle.

When he wasn't talking about his fox hunting, Tom Harrington was explaining the merits of Redbreast 12-Year-Old Single Pot Still Irish Whiskey. "Or do you like a more smokey expression in your whiskey? In that case, we'll start you off with Jameson's Black Barrel."

"You do play darts and enjoy a good cigar?" Harrington added, "I checked your record on this. Essential officer qualifications!"

Mark realized that he and Tom were becoming friends even before formally meeting. Maybe Harrington knew the importance of getting

Mark and Sarah to Dublin and keeping them close. "Yes, our folks have lined up an American preschool and elementary that looks forward to having Sarah come aboard."

When Mark asked about Mr. Gobscheit, Tom said everyone in the embassy seemed to know him, or about him at least.

"What exactly does that mean, Tom?"

"It means you won't find him riding to the hounds with us. That's merciful for the backs of the horses and all concerned."

"Anything else you can say?" Mark seemed to know what the answer would be.

"Get over here and find out. Serious stuff is going on. Your presence is needed."

CHAPTER

5

Jack Gobscheit

Jack Gobscheit would be his boss, at least in so far as Mark's cover was concerned. He was a large, thickly built, even obese, blond-haired man possessed of his authority to keep subordinates from clawing their way up to threaten him in any way. He knew this path from his long years of ascent by removing those ahead in line. He did this by seeding subtle doubts about their capacity, integrity, or performance. These doubts were wholly unfounded, but young Jack knew how to curry favor with his superiors and never to leave obvious fingerprints on the necks he slowly and maliciously compressed, in the manner of a giant yellow boa constrictor. In this way, Jack Gobscheit skirted ahead of his contemporaries and cleared his path to increased power and privilege.

Another method in his arsenal was to learn to play golf and happen upon the golfing parties of his superiors wholly by chance. He always kept a bottle of a good single malt in his golf bag, along with a number of shot glasses. All by happenstance, of course.

In this way, he learned much from his bosses' bosses and even from the very head of the organization on one or two occasions. He knew from them that someday he would need to be prepared to entertain them in his modest home and for this, he would need an attractive and intelligent wife. How to attain this goal suddenly seemed obvious one morning at the office when he noticed a smart, well-dressed secretary, who prepared his boss's correspondence. It was a bonanza of an opportunity when she seemed to respond to his self-interested glances.

Self-interest was the very persona of young Gobscheit and, as it turned out, pert Ms. Sally Cartwright, who had aspirations of her own. In fact, these mutual aspirations were at the heart of their growing relationship, though neither admitted this to the other. They were simply using their flirtation to advance themselves in the office. And when Jack was gifted by Sally with a glance at correspondence in preparation for his boss, both subtly recognized the game was on.

Of course, it had been office policy for many years to frown on, or even forbid, office dalliances. But these were changing times. Securing the intimacy of one's own lawfully wedded partner was about all one could hope for in those days. After all, even wife swapping was becoming in vogue or, at least, depicted in some popular films and imaginings.

And so, as fate would have it, one day Jack and Sally announced their betrothal to well wishes all around. The wedding was largely an office party, for which both went heavily into debt, fully realizing it was part of a grand investment in their respective futures. Even the head of the organization was invited, though he declined with a thoughtful note and small, but appropriate, gift.

The Gobscheits were now front and center on the office's radar screen. Within six months, Jack got his first promotion and today Sally is the personal assistant to one of the ministry overseers.

When Jack Gobscheit moved up from the Garda Síochána to the Defense Ministry, he was assigned a very able assistant named Fogarty Gorgarty. This man struck him in all ways as a loyal subordinate who would never engage in the schemes that propelled Jack's own career. He relied more and more on Fogarty and, since Jack preferred golfing with his cronies, left increasing amounts of the workload in his capable hands.

There was a problem with this, however, that Gobscheit didn't fully understand. Seeing how much Fogarty was accomplishing, it was only a matter of time before Jack's wife Sally saw the occasion to cautiously seduce Fogarty. This started with furtive glances and then, low and behold, sharing some of Jack's draft correspondence that found its way to her before him. In fact, Jack was so lazy that he frequently took classified documents home to have Sally help with drafting Jack's responses. And so, this went on until Sally and Fogarty started having an affair right under Jack's pronounced and somewhat magisterial nose.

While Fogarty was fond of Sally to be sure, his real motivation had nothing to do with advancing either's career in the ministry. It was simply to spy on Jack. After all, Foggy was a spy for NATO and was about to bring aboard his old friend Mark Jamison to tighten the net around Mr. Gobscheit.

Being less than totally clueless, Jack feared losing Sally and set about to increase his income to dazzle her with all that she might desire. To accomplish this, he turned to his relationship with Sergay Markov, a senior political officer of Dublin's overstaffed Russian Embassy. Gobscheit knew Markov from his days in the Garda Síochána, when the Russians needed police protection for high-level visitors from Moscow. Markov shared that his relationship with some of Putin's inner circle provided a great opportunity for both their futures. This would entail both of their participation in a hotel venture in Moscow. Putin's personal stake in the project meant the venture's certainty. The hotel would enjoy a guaranteed clientele of visiting dignitaries.

The only thing holding the deal back was getting Gobscheit to Moscow to meet the investors and gain their approval. All Gobscheit would be called upon to do, Markov assured him, was make certain this hotel would be promoted through his contacts at the various ministries and foreign legations in Dublin.

CHAPTER

6

Coming Aboard in Ireland

In May 2024, NATO's newly formed Critical Undersea Infrastructure Network held its first meeting to protect submarine cables. Fogarty Gorgarty was sent to Brussels to represent the ministry. Gobscheit felt the assignment should have been his but he was informed he was too important and needed to stay put in Dublin and monitor any political backlash from the Greens and others opposed to any Irish involvement with NATO.

Within weeks of Gorgarty's return, Gobscheit was called to a meeting with the prime minister, who informed him that an American with broad experience in naval and diplomatic matters would be added to his staff. This position would report to him, but was being added to placate NATO with how seriously Ireland was taking the matter of undersea cable security. An added benefit, the prime minister added, was that Mark

Jamison's salary would not affect Gobscheit's budget, because the Yanks were paying his freight.

Gobscheit learned from the PM that on April 6, 2021, an undersea data cable was destroyed, with evidence pointing to a Russian trawler. Seven months later, Norway's Svalbard cable was cut, with suspicious tracks left on the seabed. Then in 2023, Sweden discovered a cut cable. Gobscheit was told it looked like critical infrastructure was being surveyed and that these were possible Russian training missions. He was to put Gorgarty and Jamison on the security of Ireland's cables.

The PM made himself crystal clear. "Just one slip up, one cut cable, and Brussels will be all over us. Our beloved neutrality won't be worth a tinker's damn if NATO thinks we're not up to the job. And I sure as hell don't want any Brits over here. The American Navy is bad enough. The Royal Navy... never on your life."

Jack Gobscheit was in full agreement. He wasn't happy about having Jamison join his staff, but, on the other hand, if anything went wrong with any of Ireland's cables, he could point to Gorgarty, formerly of the Royal Navy, and Jamison, former American Navy, to leave Gobscheit and his office with a good measure of insulation. Besides, if there really was an issue with the Russians, maybe he and Markov could steer matters to their mutual benefit.

And there matters stood when Mark and Sarah Jamison arrived in Dublin and presented themselves at the US Embassy to meet with naval attaché Tom Harrington and a brief sit down for the three of them with US Ambassador Sheldon Pringle.

"So, Mark, Sarah, if there is anything at all that we can do for you here at the embassy, just let us know. I know you'll be in good hands with Tom here. Mark, any questions at all before you head over to the Defense Ministry?"

"Well, I've never been briefed on Mr. Gobscheit, the man I'm ostensibly reporting to. Anything you can say about him?"

"Just keep your antenna up and your radar switched on, Captain. You'll soon be telling us."

The ambassador thought for a moment and then suggested that Tom take Sally for coffee in his adjacent dining room.

"There are a few things you should know, Mark. Ireland faced a massive cyberattack affecting its health system two years ago. As part of the cooperative agreement with NATO, Ireland will be able to access the Cooperative Cyber Defense Center in Estonia. But there is more to it. It's not unusual to uncover spies and moles here, including at least one in Ireland's two-chamber parliament, the Oireachtas.

"Sergey Prokopiev, the Russian spy who allegedly recruited the lawmaker, was among the four Russian Embassy staff expelled from Ireland in March 2022. All were identified as members of Russia's military intelligence agency, the GRU, and engaged in espionage. But Prokopiev continued to coordinate activities with the Irish lawmaker via a female Russian agent sent periodically to Dublin to pursue a romantic liaison with the politician—a 'honey trap' designed to compromise the amorous target.

"When reporters asked whether a Russian intelligence mole was operating within the Parliament, the Irish prime minister said he couldn't confirm the information, but added: 'It shouldn't come as a surprise to any of us.'

"Efforts by Russian intelligence agents increased following Russia's invasion of Ukraine in February 2022. When Ireland expelled the Russian spies, Moscow retaliated by banning scores of Irish politicians from traveling to Russia, a move that drew more than a little humor in Dublin. The lawmaker had been recruited in 2019 as Russia sought to inflame Brexit-related tensions between Ireland and the UK, particularly in the UK region of Northern Ireland.

"It's good you're here, Mark. We are curious about Mr. Gobscheit and what goes on in his office and the ministry as a whole.

"My wife, Susie, and I look forward to hosting you and Sarah for dinner before long. Meanwhile, I have a feeling you and Tom will get on famously. Thanks very much for visiting today."

As Mark reached Ambassador Pringle's door, he heard him say in undertones, "The bastard cheats at golf."

CHAPTER

7

Jamison Meets Gobscheit

Mark had a warm reception by Foggy at the ministry. He proceeded to introduce him around to the various colleagues who would be working on undersea cable security issues.

When it came to meeting Gobscheit, the two were continuously put off, however. Gobscheit was still fuming over Gorgarty's trip to Brussels and the special way Sally avoided Jack's eyes when Foggy's name came up. Gobscheit's secretary said he was on phone calls even when the indicator lights on her desk were off. Then he was out of the office. This continued until Foggy caught him in the hallway and pressed him to meeting "our new Yank, the distinguished Mr. Jamison." At that, Jack relented and asked both to join him in five minutes. Even then, they were kept waiting for half an hour.

When they sat down together, Jack Gobscheit apologized for his busy schedule and said the office and the entire ministry were delighted that Mark would be joining them. He then offered a few pointers for their relationship.

"This office is close knit and keeps me fully apprised of anything of concern. As Fogarty knows, I hate surprises above all. And the one thing I expect above all is loyalty. And that means undivided loyalty. I know you will be close to your embassy and Ambassador Pringle. That's certainly OK. Sheldon and I are friends and frequently golf together. I can't say much for his game, but he tries his best. Just between us, I suspect he cheats. Anyway, you'll find me a fair boss in every respect. Especially if a bottle of Redbreast turns up every now and then. You know, some of it can be found that's fifty years old. Not that I drink in the office."

"At least not routinely," jibed Foggy with a smile.

"So, I'm here for you, Mark, and expect you both to keep me fully apprised of any security issues at all. You may as well know we get wind of attempts by NATO to scare us half to death from time to time. They usually dress this up with nefarious Russian misdeeds affecting our sacred cables. But between us boys, much of this turns out to be concocted by NATO to tempt us to jettison our neutrality. That will never happen. And I expect both of you and your teams to be vigilant in not allowing NATO mischief to be misread. Always be alert to the real sources of any red flags that you spot."

"Thank you very much, Mr. Gobscheit," Jamison said as he and Foggy stood up to leave.

"Jack, Jack, always Jack, Mark. Let's be informal and be friends."

"Thanks very much, Jack." Jamison then gave the few lines in Gaelic he memorized for the occasion, "Tá áthas orm a bheith ag obair leat chun sábháilteacht an domhain a chinntiú." (I'm pleased to meet you and to work together for the safety of the world.)

Jack burst out laughing and asked Foggy, "What did he just say?"

"I think he said we should memorialize our meeting with some of the Redbreast he keeps in his bottom drawer."

"OK, OK, gentlemen. Sit back down." With that, Jack produced three small glasses and the revered Redbreast. Pouring a shot for each of them, he raised his glass and said, "Slante. Welcome aboard, Mark!"

They took the drinks in one swallow, put the glasses down, and thanked Jack for the auspicious start of working together to help save the world.

On the way back to their offices, Mark looked at Foggy and said what a great fellow they were working for and what a fine relationship he observed. Foggy motioned that Mark should follow him outside. He obviously didn't feel his office was a safe place to speak candidly.

Neither Foggy nor Mark smoked cigarettes, but Foggy produced a pack in case any were wondering why they needed to speak out in the courtyard.

"He was just seen at Beshoff's on O'Connell Street with Sergay Markov from the Russian Embassy. The two are cooking something up, I'm sure of it."

"Or it could just be a friendly lunch?"

"Not a chance, Mark. Markov worked with Prokopiev as a political officer. He was one of his spies, but because he was a friend of Gobscheit, he wasn't booted out of here like the other four who were. I'm telling you, they are up to something."

"How secure is my office, Foggy? Is my secretary working for me or observing me for Gobscheit?"

"Really, a little of both. Presume the latter. Best our private conversations are like this."

Mark coughed and put out his cigarette. They both headed back inside, then closed out the day and headed home.

CHAPTER

8

Sarah Meets Mrs. Markov

"So how was your first day with your new boss?"

"I will start and then ask you the same question," responded Mark.

"My day went great with Foggy showing me around. I like my secretary and the staff was very friendly. The Irish are sure engaging and love to chat. Finally got to meet my boss and even had a whiskey toast with Foggy and him to welcome me on board. All in all, I'm very pleased with how things are starting off here. Now, how about you? How was your day at the school Tom Harrington found for you? He's quite helpful, isn't he?"

"Well, I couldn't be happier with how this is all working out. Tom is certainly wonderful and this apartment he found for us is so close to everything. Glad we don't have a car over here and my Leap Card works for DART and Luas tickets. Of course, *you* get a car and driver to take you to the ministry, you softy. But I enjoy meeting local folks on public transport."

"That's great. Tell me about the school and who you're meeting there."

"Sure. All that's going really well. The Nord Anglia International School is very highly regarded and Tom was great to organize the position for me. The principal and other teachers are very helpful. They've assigned me another teacher to share my classroom and help show me the ropes. I love that it's less demanding for paperwork than in the States. The other teacher and I hit it off right away and are already becoming friends. She has such an interesting background. You'll love meeting her. We already talked about getting the husbands together and making a foursome for dinner some evening."

"Boy, you sure don't waste any time making friends. So who is your teacher friend?"

"Elena Markov."

"Did you say Markov?"

"Yes, why? She knows everything about Dublin and has promised to take me shopping in the best places for good bargains."

"Did she tell you anything about her husband?"

"Just that he teaches part-time at Trinity College and does some consulting work with the Russian embassy. He knows about developments in Eastern Europe and is up to speed about Irish politics. I think you'll find him fascinating."

"Yes. I'm sure I will. Can't wait to meet them both. Did she say his first name?"

41

"Yes. Sergay. Sergay Markov. I'm sure you can check him out on the website for Trinity College."

"Speaking of Trinity, we may have time to catch the last of the Book of Kells exhibit. I'm told it's an incredible high-tech presentation of the contents of its famous old library. Tom Harrington says it not only boasts a digital presentation that envelopes you, but also has modern duplicates of the old statuary found inside the library. These things actually come alive and speak to you as you approach them. It should be fun."

"Ireland sure wants to show off its high-tech role. We may as well go and enjoy it," Sarah added. "I wonder if having Apple here now has anything to do with it.

"Let me get organized a bit. I guess we'll Uber over."

"Sure, that'll work," responded Mark, checking the scheduled hours for the exhibit on his Apple phone. Suddenly, it struck him that the Jamisons and Apple had both found a new home in Ireland.

CHAPTER

9

Apple Computer Comes to Ireland

Walking to the Book of Kells exhibit on the Trinity campus, Mark was thinking about the role of the undersea cables in supporting all that Apple was doing on the Emerald Isle. What a tempting prize Ireland was becoming for anyone wanting to control the high-tech treasures accumulating here. All because it was a central telecommunication hub providing vital connectivity to NATO and the free world. And maybe attracting the attention of adversaries wanting to break the link and break up NATO.

The Book of Kells experience was remarkable for both Mark and Sarah. Some exhibits offered virtual reality experiences transporting them back to the time when the Book of Kells was created, allowing them to immerse themselves in the medieval world. Augmented reality technology overlayed digital information onto the physical pages of the Book of Kells. Multimedia presentations included immersive videos, animations, and sound, to bring the Book of Kells to life and explain its historical significance.

Apple came to Ireland in the 1980s and established a major campus at Hollyhill, County Cork. This state-of-the-art facility is a major hub for Apple's operations in Europe and is home to a large team of engineers and researchers working on cutting-edge technologies.

Once the door was opened, many other high-tech companies followed Apple's lead and the welcoming policies of the Irish government. Microsoft has a significant presence in Ireland, with offices in Dublin, Cork, and Galway. Google operates a data center in Dublin and has offices in the city. Amazon has a number of facilities in Ireland, including data centers and fulfillment centers in Dublin, Cork, and Athlone. IBM has a large presence in Ireland, with offices in Dublin, Cork, and Galway. Intel has a major manufacturing facility in Leixlip, County Kildare.

Ireland's importance quickly spread to pharmaceuticals and cutting-edge medical devices. Pfizer has a major research and development center in Dublin. Merck has a manufacturing facility in Carlow. AbbVie has a research and development center in Dublin, as does AstraZeneca. Medtronic has a major manufacturing facility in Galway. Boston Scientific has a manufacturing facility in Galway. Edwards Life Sciences has a manufacturing facility in Galway.

The country's competitive tax regime, skilled workforce, strategic location and, perhaps above all, its connectedness, have made it an attractive destination for technology companies from around the world.

"So how is it," Mark wondered to himself, walking back with Sarah to an Uber stop, "that we appear prepared to go to war to defend the technology and manufacturing centers on Taiwan, and little mention is made of Ireland? Are the Silicon Docks along the River Liffey in Dublin's Docklands area so much less important than Taipei's Xinyi District? The US has committed itself to defending Taiwan. Without NATO membership, would Ireland be as readily defended?"

The example of Ukrainian suffering wouldn't be extinguished from Jamison's mind. Neutral Norway and Sweden were quick to come aboard. What about the vital telecommunication link joining the USA and Europe that is at the heart of NATO?

CHAPTER

10

GUGI

The General Staff Main Directorate for Deep Sea
Research (transcribed as Glavnoye upravlenie
glubokovodnikh issledovanii or GUGI) is a closely
guarded Russian unit that operates surface vessels,
submarines, and naval drones. Among the purposes
of GUGI is sabotage of allied undersea critical
infrastructure.

GUGI has submarines that can reach depths
of 6,000 meters. They are equipped with tools,
cameras, and lighting in order to carry out
operations there. It has more than fifty ships,
submarines, and floating dry docks, which hide
submarines from satellites. NATO has photos of
some of its deep submersibles showing arms with
large cutting tools attached to them.

The report Jamison and Gorgarty were
discussing concluded as follows: "We are concerned
about heightened Russian naval activity worldwide
and that Russia's decision calculus for damaging US
and allied undersea critical infrastructure may be

changing." Determining just what that evolving calculus entails was the job that both of them were assigned to do.

Helping steer the Irish Defense Ministry toward recommending a closer relationship with NATO and leading Ireland to NATO membership was their sub rosa agenda. Removing or discrediting obstacles in their way was among their tasks.

As for Mr. Gobscheit, keeping Sally Cartright as his contented wife and adding to his eventual retirement package comprised the core of his agenda. The latter included a sizable share of income from a Moscow hotel venture facilitated by Sergay Markov, which required a level of accommodation to matters Russian or at least neutral in the face of various provocations.

And so matters stood, until one day a senior member of the leadership of GUGI was reported in contact with Mr. Gobscheit's office. The call was routed to him from the Russian Embassy, with junior staff members speaking fluent Russian monitoring and translating on both ends of the call.

All of Ireland had been alerted to the enormous series of storms that broke out unexpectedly in the North Atlantic and gathered abruptly off the Irish west coast. As the orange warnings turned to red, all ships were ordered into the nearest ports and disaster alerts were issued across much of the Emerald Isle.

There was one ship that found itself in a serious predicament. Actually, there were two. The surface vessel was a Russian trawler in the employ of GUGI. It was unfortunately tethered to a deep submersible as the storm quickly and unexpectedly rose in furiousness. The tether had to be removed and the mission called off while both vessels looked to find safe harbor.

The difficulty would be hard for the Russians to relate and Jamison and Gorgarty were quickly summoned to listen in and then give their expert takes on the call.

Ostensibly, the call asked for safe harbor for both craft at Portmagee. That was quickly approved. But there was something else that was conveyed. The submersible was on a retrieval mission for a lost, highly technical device that needed to be kept confidential. Neither the incoming trawler nor the submersible it carried could be boarded or inspected in any way. The Russians were providing the coordinates for an area they wanted kept safe from any intrusion until they could return to the area and find the device.

Deputy Minister Jack Gobscheit said he would need to consult his superiors, but would assure immediate safe harbor and no boarding on the vessels. The storm was so bad, he shared, that no vessel, Irish or otherwise, would dare venture out to the area described. The call ended cordially and a follow-up call for the next day was arranged.

Jamison and Gorgarty were asked to consult on the situation and return with their initial opinion within half an hour. Jamison took a deep breath when he realized the coordinates encircled the area of the AE6 relay boosting station on that major cable.

"Foggy, are you aware of what we found there? What the device is or very well may be?"

"Mark, you are going to say it's a nuke, aren't you? NATO clued me in just a few weeks ago."

"Well, unless I miss my guess, they may have been swapping out the device with one with recharged tritium. Based on the situational reports I'm seeing from the States and from Brussels, they may have also been replacing it with a larger yield device to ensure a sufficient magnetic pulse to knock out the sending and receiving stations up and down Ireland's west coast. That would put America's East Coast and Europe in for a tailspin, destroy Ireland's high-tech hub for a very long time, and send NATO into crisis mode. If it was joined with other undersea attacks and maybe knocking out a satellite or two, the lights go off for a very long time."

"Long enough for Moscow to build its bridge to Kaliningrad right over Poland?"

"Yep, that's what I'm thinking. Now, what do we tell Gobscheit? I have to alert Tom Harrington immediately. You know Jack far better than I do. Can you explain as much or as little of this that you think he needs to know?"

"It won't be easy. I'll do my best and tell him we consulted. I'll let you know how it goes."

CHAPTER

11

Take a Letter

Following Gorgarty's briefing, Jack had no option but to alert his minister and, with her, Ireland's prime minister. After all, a nuclear device may be missing in Irish waters. The response Jack received was to follow up with the Russian Embassy and give the Russians everything they ask for.

"We are not equipped to do anything else right now and don't want to get NATO or the damned Americans involved, at least until we have to. Jack," his minister told him, "you get on this personally. I don't care if we need to send you to Moscow to meet personally with Lavrov or whoever Putin has entrusted with this mess. Hell, use our embassy to see about a meeting with old Vladimir himself."

Hearing this, Jack's mind raced. He couldn't believe his good fortune. "Wait until I tell Markov that I can finally meet the other hotel investors. Maybe even Putin himself!"

Of course, he would have to sort out the matter of the nuclear device, but maybe it would all be cleared up before he got to Moscow. The thing he had to focus on was keeping this from the Yanks and NATO for as long as possible.

Meanwhile, Tom Harrington was ecstatic. "Jamison, do you realize how important this is? You've been at it for so short a time and you may already have found us a real treasure."

Harrington phoned him back an hour later. "Mark, ONI wants you out there to photograph as much of the trawler and submersible as possible. Get out there right away."

"Tom, are you crazy? Roads are closed. At least those that haven't washed out. Portmagee is so damned remote. It's near the heart of the storm. And how will I get near the vessels. Where will I stay? Everything must be boarded up by now."

"Take a letter to Garcia."

"Tom, what did you just say?"

"Take a letter to Garcia. You know what it means."

"Yes, dammit I do, Tom. Tell ONI that I'm on it."

"And you can bet we'll have one of our subs combing the area by the time you get there. Assurances from the Irish government mean nothing to us."

So, on his way home, Jamison mused at Tom's meaning. Andrew Rowan was a US Army courier tasked with delivering a letter to General

Garcia during the Spanish-American War. Rowan's mission was perilous, requiring him to cross the sea and travel many miles through hostile territory to find a general whose location was constantly changing. Despite the challenges, Rowan completed his mission without complaint or hesitation. The story is used by the Naval Academy to tell those who would lead that they must first carry out orders by taking initiative to overcome obstacles. The phrase "Take a letter to Garcia" has since become a metaphor for someone who is willing to go above and beyond their duties and complete a difficult task without detailed guidance or complaint.

Mark explained to Sarah that she should call his office in the morning and explain he was too ill to come in. Foggy would help her concoct something. Meanwhile, he had to head out in the morning through the perilous storm and find his way through the pouring horizontal rain all the way across to the very land's end of the west coast, to a promontory sticking out into the swirling Atlantic.

"Sounds like Valentia Island."

"Yep, you guessed it, or as close as possible without needing a boat or bridge, Portmagee."

"Where will you stay? Everything is probably closed down because of the horrible weather."

"You know, I stayed in an old double-decker bus once. And found my way into unlocked old boats on the dock. Don't worry about me. I'll need the extra battery charger for my iPhone and lots of foul-weather gear. And your camera please."

"But how will you get there? Your driver only takes you to the office."

"Uber!"

CHAPTER

12

Portmagee

The drive across Ireland in the middle of a red-alert storm was about as frightening as it was slow going. The worst wasn't the detours or even the huge puddles where Mark was sure the car was going to stall out and they would need to walk in the downpour.

Blessings on this Uber driver who pushed on in spite of it all. Maybe it was his nerves or just Irish gregariousness on steroids, but the man wouldn't shut up. Mark had to feign sleeping, but when the car jumped coming out of a deep puddle, the driver knew Mark was faking and continued uninterrupted.

On the way, they came to Cork and needed to rest and eat. Mark suggested they find the modern Apple Cork campus, with its 6,000 employees, but everything was shut down because of the deluge. The intrepid Uber driver and Mark ate dreadful things at the few gas stations that remained open.

On the drive, Jamison recalled Dmitry Medvedev, the deputy chairman of Russia's Security Council, issuing a stark warning a few months earlier.

The undersea cables that enable global communications had become a legitimate target for Russia, he had said. Medvedev's warning came after Nord Stream 2, a pipeline that transfers gas from Russia to Germany, was blown up. Russian officials believed the West had been involved in the attack. "If we proceed from the proven complicity of Western countries in blowing up the Nord Streams, then we have no constraints—even moral—left to prevent us from destroying the ocean floor cable communications of our enemies." Medvedev had posted this on Telegram. It was pretty clear why Mark was summoned to help.

Mark knew all about that bombing and what really was involved. It was hard keeping silent about it and so much else. Someday he would disclose a great deal writing in novels that disguised reality as fiction. Hopefully, some readers would notice. Mark nodded off and then fell into a deep sleep.

He came to with the snoring of the Uber driver, who was fast asleep in the front seat. They were on the side of the road and the rain seemed to be letting up, but not the snoring. Mark had to let the poor man sleep, so he pulled his coat up around his ears and fell back into a deep sleep. In his dream, he was welcomed aboard an ornate submarine, with Captain Nemo playing the organ in his grand salon. This Nemo spoke Russian and had beautiful women in attendance. Then it wasn't a submarine, but a starship heading through deep space.

Suddenly, the driver woke him saying they were at Portmagee and the storm was continuing to let up. The one inn facing the port was actually open and had rooms for both Mark and the driver.

***

In the morning, Jamison saw the crew of the trawler busying itself on the deck. The submersible appeared to be a drone that was hoisted on and lashed down on the deck.

Jamison got dressed and grabbed his phone, slipped Sarah's camera into his pocket, and headed out the door, taking pictures like some oblivious tourist. The crew waved to him to stop and he waved back saying good morning and that the pancakes at the inn were superb.

The letter to Garcia was on its way to delivery. Mark quickly messaged the photos to Captain Tom Harrington at the embassy and then headed back inside the inn to phone Foggy and check in with all that would be going on at the ministry.

CHAPTER

13

An Unexpected Voyage

Foggy was clearly animated during their phone conversation. Thanks to both of them, NATO was fully apprised of the situation and the story quickly broke in the *Irish Times*. Parliamentary figures were livid that this could be happening and the ministry put Gobscheit up as their point person, saying he had been engaged in quiet diplomacy with the Russians for a full accounting of the matter and that Ireland's security and safety would never be compromised.

Foggy also related that Gobscheit called in his Green Party friends and told them they couldn't rule out NATO mischief over the whole matter. Gobscheit told them NATO was pushing hard to get Ireland to surrender its precious neutrality and come aboard with them, but that this would never be allowed to happen. When pressed for details, Jack went so far as to say that he suspected the new American expert assigned to his office might actually be there for NATO as much as Ireland. He told them and the press that Ireland must be vigilant with both Russia and NATO.

"Wait a second," Jamison said. "Did Jack mention me by name?"

"In background and off the record, he did."

"Then I'm totally screwed. The Russians will know who is taking pictures of them..." Those were the last words anyone but the Russians on the trawler heard from Jamison, as they headed back out to sea with him locked securely aboard.

It would be up to Foggy now to sort the mess out. Mark might be in serious trouble in Portmagee. Foggy called his NATO contacts and was told satellite surveillance showed the trawler heading back out into the Atlantic. He called the inn and was told a driver arrived to take Mark back to Dublin. The innkeeper said it looked like a number of folks were waiting for them outside, but he didn't see them get into a vehicle. Instead, it looked like they were headed off toward the docks.

Meanwhile, in the office, Gobscheit was grilling Foggy for the leaks to NATO and the press. He threatened Mr. Gorgarty in no uncertain terms of his future assignments if any of this mess could be traced back to him or his friend Jamison. And where was Jamison? Jack demanded to know. Foggy could only say he was trying to find out.

It was only a few minutes later that Gobscheit was summoned to the minister's office. "What the hell is going on, Jack? The Russian Embassy just reported that an American spy was found on one of their ships that we promised safe harbor and sanctuary to. They are beyond livid!"

All Jack could say is that his folks were trying to sort out the situation and that Jamison may have been planted on his staff to stir up this mess on behalf of NATO.

"On behalf of NATO? Jack, it looks like the Russians have gifted us with a loose nuke in our waters. One that may be near to a key cable for all of the free world. I think we may be needing NATO's help now, no? Anyway, we can't very well keep them away under the circumstances. When Jamison turns up, I want to see both of you back in my office."

"What about my going to Moscow to sort this out? The Russian ambassador had little to say because he was not briefed and said the sensitivity of the matter probably meant he would not be anytime soon."

The minister's anger was growing. "Alright, Jack. You make the arrangements and go to Moscow. I'll tell the press that we have sent our best man to sort this mess out and keep us safe. Do you think you'll be able to do that?"

Jack provided his assurances and said he would depart in the morning with two junior Russian speakers from his staff.

"No, Jack. All your staff stays. Our embassy in Moscow will provide translators and anything else you need. Right? Got it?"

"Yes, of course, ma'am."

"Don't make me reassign you to Fisheries. Good luck then."

CHAPTER

14

Flying High

Jack Gobscheit would soon be flying high. Thanks to the minister's instructions, he was free to have Sergay Markov join him on his flight so they could further plan out their hotel project before arriving at the Sheremetyevo Alexander S. Pushkin International Airport. Markov would take care of the high-level visits that the Irish embassy couldn't. So that would resolve the possibility of a missing nuke issue as well. If all went well enough, Jack could return home a hero with a future of great wealth. Those idiots pushing NATO down the throat of Ireland wouldn't stand a chance because Mr. Gobscheit could resolve everything better than those bozos in Brussels. He liked the sound of that and spoke it out loud to Markov while they were both sipping cocktails.

"Bozos in Brussels." They both laughed, got sloshed, and had a snoring session on the way to Moscow.

Meanwhile, back on terra firma in Dublin, Foggy and Tom Harrington were more than a bit frantic. Tom had to explain to Sarah that it appeared Mark was being detained and was now probably at sea on a Russian ship. He could say nothing further, but promised that the American embassy and State Department would soon be weighing in to secure his release. Ambassador Pringle was providing assurances to the defense minister and parliamentary leaders that Jamison was not a spy and was in Ireland to provide his naval expertise on undersea matters for the ministry. Pringle was also briefing Washington and Brussels on an hourly basis. The media was all over the matter and speculation ran high that Ireland's security was now entirely in the hands of Deputy Minister Gobscheit on his way to Moscow.

**

Jack Gobscheit's reception in Moscow went beyond Jack's expectations. The Irish ambassador himself was awaiting Jack in the embassy limousine, with press crowding nearby. The ambassador and Gobscheit briefed each other on what they knew and what they needed to know. Meetings were arranged with the Russian foreign ministry. Ireland was holding back issuing a formal protest to the Russian government until Jack could advise, following his efforts with the Russians, which would commence that evening. Meanwhile, blogging speculation was going into high gear that a huge bomb was missing near Portmagee that could devastate half of the Emerald Isle. All eyes were on Jack and Ireland was literally holding its breath on the outcome of his meetings.

But the meetings the Irish embassy arranged were with relatively low-level officials at the Russian foreign and defense ministries. No real answers or progress were forthcoming, as the security associated with GUGI reached to the highest levels. Back at his hotel, Jack phoned Sergay Markov, who was expecting to hear from him. Things would need to be elevated and Markov was on it.

"Get a good night's rest, my friend. Tomorrow may be more special than you imagine!" Markov closed.

***

The next morning, Jack phoned his ambassador to say discussions would continue at higher levels. Markov arrived with a car and driver to take Jack to his next meeting. But they were heading back to the airport, and Jack was temporarily confused.

"Don't worry, Jack. This will be a strictly domestic flight. Someone is very anxious to meet you."

The next flight was from the other side of the airport and from a private hangar.

"Have you had your breakfast yet, Jack? I think we will be dining well on this flight," Markov said as they walked up the steps to a private aircraft with engines turning over. In a few moments, both were knocking back some very cold vodka to wash down Caspian Sea caviar and trays of delicacies.

"I have learned there is much more to our hotel project, Jack. In a few hours, a great deal will be revealed to us both. So, how do you like our Russian hospitality?" Markov inquired, pointing to the shapely attendants in very short skirts. "They want us to enjoy this flight."

CHAPTER

15

Back in Dublin

"Think about it, Fogarty," Captain Tom Harrington offered on his drop by meeting at the ministry. "Russia relies significantly less on subsea cables than either the United States or NATO since it's a continental power. Its internet connectivity to Europe and Central Asia goes by land. Since Russia is less vulnerable to disruptions in subsea cable infrastructure, it's more willing to exploit our vulnerabilities. Russia, China, and Iran are all connected up safely on land."

"I know it. Most folks here don't really grasp that nearly all military secrets get passed along through these underwater cables. Encrypted sure, but still vulnerable."

"So how is the office doing without Gobscheit on the scene?" Tom asked.

"I think our main NATO skeptic is gone at the right time."

"So are you the acting deputy minister now?"

"I think so, although the SOB has never made clear the hierarchy around here. He's too afraid of getting someone competent to undercut him or compete with him."

"That's really not so unusual in any bureaucracy I've ever known."

"Tom, what do we do about Mark?" Foggy asked despairingly. "I feel terrible getting him over here to Ireland now."

"*You* feel terrible. *I'm* the one who sent him off to Portmagee and have to hold Sarah's hand through all this."

"Yeah, and I've got to deal with Sally Cartwright, who wants more of me with Gobscheit away."

"Don't tell me you're still seeing her?"

"I can't very well break it off. She's still providing me with solid intel. For God and country, you know. But now that Jack's away, she wants me to really cut his legs off and suggest to the press that he's the NATO plant."

"You mean, instead of the Russian one you suspect him being," added Tom.

"Yep. It gets complicated."

"And I'm the happy bachelor these days. You should come out riding with me when all this shit settles down. I want you to meet Seamus McGrath and the fox hunters he assembles. We'll get Mark with us, for sure. When he's safely returned to us."

"From your lips..."

"Ambassador Pringle is working with Washington to demand his immediate release. The Russians are playing dumb so far and say we planted a spy aboard one of their most sensitive ships."

"So they're admitting their trawler is picking up a lot more than Irish herring. Do you think Gobscheit in Moscow can be helpful? He's an idiot but can get lucky from time to time."

"We'd better hope your guy gets lucky this time."

***

At her preschool, Sarah was keeping her ears open. Elena Markov told her that Sergay was recalled suddenly to Moscow for consultations. She wondered if it had to do with the trap NATO was setting for the Irish.

"Trust me, Sarah, Russia would never place a nuclear weapon outside our own borders. Look where you Americans have them."

"Well, Elena, I do recall some concern about what your country put in Cuba a while back."

"Of course, but that was the old Soviet Union. We are entirely different today. Maybe we should change the subject and discuss the kids and parents' day coming up in a few weeks."

"Yes, let's do that," Sarah said, wondering about how her husband was being treated. He was never happy in rough seas, she recalled, even aboard our best American ships, let alone on an old Russian trawler.

CHAPTER

16

All at Sea

Jamison was out of touch with the world and kept in a dark hold. As the craft crawled its way through the still rough seas, he was totally miserable. There was nothing he could do except follow the instructions of the crew. But what would happen when they got to where the device was lost and an American submarine was found loitering there instead?

He wanted to strangle Foggy and Tom for getting him into this mess. He was so sorry for Sarah to be caught up in yet another misadventure. All of the escape tricks he learned over the years would be worthless. There was no one to cajole into releasing him. He knew he was now in the clutches of one of the most ruthless people on the planet: Vladimir Putin. He also knew ransoms would not be paid to any organization, much less an official part of the Russian secret service. There were no prisoner swaps he could think of, nothing to do but...oh no, his vertigo was being triggered in the dark moving hold. Now he went from bad to much worse and had to find a way to at least focus on the horizon. He lost all composure and started to pound madly on the door.

Finally, the door was opened enough for him to beg for fresh air and being let up on deck. When he saw the food that was being delivered to him, he puked. A few minutes later, a GUGI officer who spoke perfect English came to his door.

"We know who you are now, Mark Jamison. Get a hold of yourself. You are a naval officer like us who follows the orders of his government. We respect that. We can't have you looking so miserable. Let's get you to see our doctor and clean you up. He'll give you some Dramamine. Then we can sit down for a proper meal together and maybe figure out what to do with you."

Jamison didn't speak but followed the officer carefully through the shifting passageway, grabbing hold of things when everything continued to spin. At the makeshift infirmary, he was greeted by someone holding a very long needle with a drop of liquid coming out the end.

"Nyet! Nyet!" Jamison screamed.

"Calm down," the GUGI officer said. "This is the dose you need. Don't worry. Half the crew needs it from time to time."

"But I can't be sedated with Sodium Pentothal or the new stuff you folks have. I am committed to never disclose some things. I'm sure you are too."

"Yes, yes. We know all about that. Listen, Jamison, this ship is not equipped for interrogations. We collect information electronically, as you know. We don't waterboard or waste our time with that nonsense. We have no truth serums, or whatever you might think. This is to help you. I promise."

Jamison considered his options. He could run away and probably fall over with his vertigo. He was in no position to do much of anything. So he thought for a moment and said, "Do you ever need this stuff? Maybe a small dose for you first?"

"It's harmless, Captain Jamison, I assure you. But if it will help you..." The officer spoke in Russian to the medic, who injected a portion of the IV into the officer, then wiped the needle with alcohol and offered the rest to Jamison.

"One last thing. Two questions for you. What's your name and what's for dinner?" Jamison asked as he was injected.

"Stavrov and pot roast, in that order."

Jamison hoped Stavrov didn't have a communicable disease, but wasn't going to worry about it. He looked healthy enough. In less time than he could have thought possible, Mark's head stopped spinning and he felt great.

"What's in that stuff?"

"I don't know the formula. Just that it works. We can't afford to have our techs at the rail vomiting. Why don't you join me in my stateroom until dinner's ready?"

Jamison realized he really had no choice in the matter, but was grateful for his cure.

CHAPTER

17

Gelendzhik

Jack Gobscheit and Sergay Markov had enjoyed the flight immensely and were now in a limousine heading to Cape Idokopas, near the village of Praskoveyevka. They were on the Black Sea coast of Russia near Gelendzhik, Krasnodar Krai. Markov was beaming. "Few people are ever invited here."

Once inside the modern palace, they both passed through a detection scan, removed their shoes, and stepped into special slippers with antibacterial, antiviral, and antifungal properties. A light mist was also felt over their heads.

"I was told to expect this," Markov said. "Every guest at President Putin's private dacha goes through this."

"Will I meet him?" Gobscheit asked.

"Jack, he's been waiting to meet you for some time. Yes, of course you will."

They were escorted into a huge, informal gray-stone paneled room with large brown leather chairs. Beside each was a small table with a glass and bottle of sparkling water. As soon as they sat, about a half dozen gentlemen entered the room. Markov sprang to his feet and motioned for Gobscheit to stand next to him.

"These are the other investors I spoke about." Everyone spoke in Russian and made introductions. To each Jack said, "Priyatno poznakomit'sya." That was the total extent of his Russian, and from his pronunciation of "pleased to meet you", they knew immediately that he would know nothing of the conversation unless Markov cared to share things with him. It would be much less than translation; more like selective inclusion.

Once seated, one of the group started by outlining the hotel deal. There would be thirteen properties across Russia, from Moscow to Vladivostok. The group would start with three... two in Moscow and one in Saint Petersburg, which would raise the funds to eventually include the rest.

Gobscheit was beyond delighted. He and Markov had assumed it would be only a single hotel in Moscow. The group was discussing the sources of funding and interests each would have in the project. Markov kept telling Gobscheit only, "It's good, Jack. It's much better than we expected. There will be an immediate return."

Jack sat ignorantly sipping on his sparkling water when suddenly the double doors opened and everyone jumped to their feet with the entry of Vladimir Vladimirovich Putin. Jack expected him to make the rounds of greeting and shaking hands, but instead he immediately sat down and started speaking.

After a few moments, Jack looked at Sergay expectantly. "What's he saying?"

Markov whispered, "It's now thirty-one hotels across Russia, Turkey, Cyprus, Saudi Arabia, the Gulf, and Israel. And they will have casinos, the big money earners!"

"My God," whispered Jack, pretending to follow what Putin was saying.

This went on for about twenty minutes, then Putin stood, thanked the group for coming, and said he would always be available to the investors. He smiled and said it was a busy time for him and left.

To Jack's amazement, the others quickly filed past him and Markov. They abruptly also left the room, closing the doors behind them.

"What just happened, Sergay? Is there anything we are supposed to do now? I never intended we'd be committing ourselves to anything so vast... thirty-one hotels. My God," Jack repeated.

After five minutes or so that seemed an eternity, an attendant came in the room and said that the president would expect both of them to join him for dinner later that evening. For now, they were at liberty to relax for the remaining hour or so before they would be called.

Jack looked at this watch and told Markov he would need to call his minister right away and give her a report. Markov said he would take a visit to the bathroom.

Jack reported to the minister that he was negotiating directly with President Putin. He said that Putin sent his best compliments to the Irish president, parliament, and to the minister personally. He said Putin wished to thank her for making her deputy available for this important matter.

Jack said negotiations were proceeding and that he had demanded immediate removal of any Russian device of any kind from Irish waters or near any cables on the seabed. He also demanded an apology and the immediate release of Mark Jamison who was assigned to his office. Finally, Jack said he would be dining with the president that evening and would have further details to report following that.

"Jack, how did he strike you? I mean, this is a real coup for you and for the ministry. Pull this one off, Jack, and there will be no more talk of Fisheries, I assure you. I will phone the PM and pass this along. Call me no matter how late it gets after your dinner."

"Yes, of course, ma'am. Speak to you later."

Gobscheit's meeting was immediately leaked to the media and the minister was interviewed several times. The commentators all said something to the effect that all of Ireland and Europe are holding its breath. Jack couldn't imagine that "Gobscheit" was now a household word across Ireland, in European capitals, and even in Washington, DC. Even the US president asked if that could be anyone's real name.

CHAPTER

18

Jamison at Sea

Stavrov was pretty good at backgammon, though all the while keeping a wary eye on his captive. Dinner was not bad, but the hostile stares of the higher-ranked crew members in the dining room were certainly off-putting. The seas were calming a bit.

When he heard frantic steps outside in the passageway, everyone looked alarmed. Stavrov was called out for an urgent message from Moscow. Jamison felt it had to concern his fate aboard the vessel. He was tempted to make a run for it, but run where? Stavrov was probably receiving word that Jamison should have weights tied to his ankles and be tossed overboard to delight the sharks. He wasn't sure what to think or do.

Time seemed frozen as Jamison sat silently, awaiting his fate.

When Stavrov entered, everyone looked at him expectantly. Were their knives to be sharpened to cut this American up for the smaller fish? Stavrov looked around the room and then stared coldly at Jamison before breaking into a smile. "Get this Yank some dessert. The Kremlin says to treat him well before we drop him at the next port."

Jamison didn't know how to react. He searched Stavrov's face for any sign this was a cruel joke. Then he asked if the ship could arrange a phone call to his wife, who must be worried silly.

"Moscow says foreign spies should pay 1,000 rubles for a phone call." Everyone laughed except Jamison.

"Yeah, sure. Anything else you desire?"

"Well, a bed would be welcome. And what about another of those shots?"

This last part, Stavrov translated for the others present and received hearty laughter. "Yes, sometimes the crew fakes sea sickness just to get the shots. Now you know why I didn't refuse to get jabbed with some of yours."

The call with Sarah was a huge relief to them both.

"Mark, your boss flew all the way to Moscow to fight for your freedom. He demanded to speak directly with Putin. And he did it, Mark. Mr. Gobscheit did it! You're going to be coming home safe and sound. I am so grateful, I don't really know what to say."

Well, that confirmed why Mark got dessert and was allowed this phone call home. Maybe the poor picture Foggy had painted of his boss was totally unfair. Mark couldn't wait to get back and thank Gobscheit in person.

Stavrov told Mark he would need to stay locked below decks in a stateroom the following day while a package down on the sea floor got located and retrieved.

"The submersible you photographed will get put back into action. We can't let you see any of that. If all goes well, the following day we'll head for Galway Bay and a rendezvous with the Garda Cósta na hÉireann, the Irish Coast Guard. Maybe your wife can meet you there."

"Sounds like a plan," Jamison responded. He secretly hoped his navy hadn't located the lost device so these Russians could retrieve it and hurry him off the trawler and back to Sarah.

CHAPTER

19

Dinner with Vladimir Vladimirovich

As they were led for what seemed like half a mile through this very large complex, Jack was all over Sergay for the proper protocol expected at dinner. "Beats me," was all Markov could muster. "No one I know has ever made it this far, let alone all the way to his private dining room."

The protocol was made clear when they joined President Putin. He would propose toasts and speak. They would listen. When they felt it appropriate to speak, he would speak over them. Thus, the meal and conversation were actually enjoyable. They could focus on the food, drink, and just listening. And he asked Markov to translate accurately or he would speak in English if necessary.

He started with a continuation of the hotel project and its anticipated yield over the years, which would be safely deposited with codes that no one could interfere with. The oligarchs that they both met were providing some of the startup funding and the Russian state would guarantee the necessary loans. He assured them that many wanted in on this project, but he had limited outsiders to just the two of them.

What did the group want in return? What would Gobscheit's contribution be? Just to keep Ireland neutral and free and to keep the ravenous NATO SOBs at bay. "So you see," Putin explained, staring into Jack's eyes, "our interests are identical. I love a free and independent Ireland and I know you do too." Jack nodded his head enthusiastically.

"And I know we have some issues that need to be sorted out this evening. We shall do that," the president of the Russian Federation added.

"Let's talk about the device you want gone from Irish waters. I will be happy to remove it and some others you may be unaware of. I will also make sure your man Jamison is safely returned to you. I have already had the ship he's on alerted to take good care of him.

"Now these undersea cables that are so important break and frequently need repair. Unlike what NATO is saying, we don't want to disrupt them or damage them in any way. We want to protect them. After all, the entire world depends on the cables that reach your country.

"Please listen carefully. Since 2021, the USA has created what it calls the Cable Security Fleet, which, I assure you, involves the Pentagon. SubCom, one of the world's largest subsea fiber-optic cable developers for telecommunication and technology firms, is the sole cable contractor for the US military. It was awarded a $10 million annual contract to operate the fleet, which consists of two US flagged and crewed cable ships, the *CS Dependable* and *CS Decisive*, which are required to be available for laying, maintaining, and repairing critical cables.

"It should not come as a surprise that we prefer a more neutral repair plan, one centered where it should rightfully be... in your country.

"I think we can arrange an Irish cable protection fleet to inspect and maintain the undersea cables. Wouldn't that be better than the Pentagon sticking its nose everywhere?

"And I think you, Jack Gobscheit, Deputy Director of the Defense Ministry of Ireland, are precisely the person to undertake this effort and get it through your parliament."

Vladimir Vladimirovich changed his expression completely and took a long sip of his red wine.

"So how's the dinner, Jack, Sergay? You know this wine is produced locally."

"Really fabulous," Jack said in English. "The best I've enjoyed in many years. May I respond to you in English?"

"Yes, of course," responded Putin, glancing at Sergay to convey his help could be necessary.

"Mr. President, I think your ideas are perfectly in line with my own thinking. It will take our cooperating to avoid NATO provocations. I know Russia poses no threat to us and isn't asking us to join anything that would surrender our neutrality. And I want to thank you for taking the steps you indicated at the outset. Yes... fully yes to your proposal with a few conditions."

"Go ahead. What are they?"

"That our understanding is never revealed, that the costs of these repair ships are minimal and, most importantly... that we get together for dinner more often!" With that, Jack raised his glass and said, "Zah zdah-rohv-yuh," which Putin, smiling, repeated.

"You know, Jack," Putin added, "someday we think you are going to be the prime minister." They toasted again, with Jack's face reddened by the alcohol and emotion. He fought the urge to stand and move to embrace his new best friend, Vladimir Vladimirovich.

CHAPTER

20

The Celebrity

Jack Gobscheit didn't know it, but he was heading for a hero's reception back home. The minister portrayed his negotiation as a great win for Ireland and a demonstration that it was on top of its own security affairs. At the same time, Sally Cartwright had been interviewed saying she felt sure he was doing it for NATO. Of course, despite Fogarty's protestations of her scheme, her motivation in doing so was to undercut Jack and promote Foggy. But it all worked out incredibly well for Mr. Gobscheit.

The Greens were delighted he was safekeeping Irish waters while preserving neutrality of the Emerald Isle. Any suspicions about possible NATO motivations were quickly subordinated to the favorable outcome. NATO could not say for certain he was not doing it for them. Some in Brussels were even tempted to take credit for the operation. In any event, NATO and Ireland were beside themselves with admiration for this heretofore relatively unknown figure from the Defense Ministry bureaucracy. All agreed his motivations were secondary to ridding the waters of lurking Russian threats.

And so, the hero's reception was also provided by his loving wife Sally Cartwright, who now regretted any indiscretions with Fogarty, whom she now considered a nobody. Any reference to her comments to the press were covered over as the media's confusion of what she was saying about her very distinguished and all-Irish husband. None of that NATO stuff for him or them.

The minister phoned him to take the next few days off with his family. In truth, she didn't want him competing with her for media attention at the office.

"Was the device safely located and removed?" the press asked.

"Yes, we have every reason to believe it was," she replied.

"Was your deputy, Jack Gobscheit, the one who achieved this?"

"Yes. Of course, he was acting for the ministry under my explicit directions."

"Did you arrange the meeting directly with Putin? Have you ever worked with him?"

"Our embassy in Moscow made all the arrangements. I have not myself negotiated with President Putin, but have always held myself out as ready to do so, as the prime minister may direct."

"Do you consider him a hero for accomplishing this?"

"I think the entire nation is relieved and most grateful to our Mr. Gobscheit. We, of course, express our gratitude to President Putin as well, especially for clearing up any misunderstanding related to the role of the American Captain Mark Jamison, also on my staff. He is due to come home shortly and is with his wife in Galway for a few days away from the spotlight."

"Thank you, Minister."

"Thank you all for your accurate reporting on this matter. Ireland is safe and secure once more."

The camera lights were turned off and the minister settled back to field inquiries from the prime minister. Today, NATO and even the Pentagon were phoning and questioning her. Her labradoodle, resting behind her imposing red desk chair, was tested for its calming influence in these past few days. She hoped he would continue to do so, but had her doubts.

CHAPTER

21

The Jamisons Return

Tom Harrington joined Sarah at the Galway docks. They stood together awaiting Mark's return on the Irish Coast Guard vessel that collected him from the trawler several miles out at sea. When the moment arrived to step ashore, Mark looked relatively calm and collected as he hugged Sarah and ignored Tom.

"Look, Mark, I'm sorry I sent you out there to Portmagee, but ONI directed me. It was a vital opportunity to see what the Russians were doing and what their submersible looked like."

They all climbed into the chauffeured limousine that Ambassador Pringle thoughtfully lent to his naval attaché for the occasion. "Take my car and find out what the hell went on during the drive back to Dublin," were the ambassador's instructions to Tom. But Mark continued to ignore him until they crossed into County Kildare and Sarah begged him to forgive Tom.

"He was just following his orders, like you always do," Sarah admonished him.

"Take a letter to Garcia. That really took the cake. Talk about sending someone out into one of the worst storms on record and giving no backup or protection. And the trawler's crew were already there and waiting. This place is a leaky sieve. They had to know I was coming."

"We don't know that," Tom responded.

"Well, I take it you received the photos I messaged. Did they satisfy ONI?"

"You bet. They were great, Mark. Job well done. They will probably have a letter or ribbon for you at some point."

"Swell, that's just what this retired consultant or spy or whocver the hell I am wants."

"Well, everyone up the chain was pleased, Mark."

"Yeah. How about you, Sarah?"

Sarah turned to look dismissively at Tom. "Please don't ever do anything like that again, Tom. Promise. We are getting too old for this kind of excitement."

"Promise," Tom said sheepishly. "Never again."

"Or we're both on the next flight out of here, orders or no orders," Mark chimed in.

"Got it."

"OK." Mark turned to Tom and they shook hands.

"Listen, to help make this up to you, come on the ride this weekend. You'll both be my guests with Seamus McGrath and the fox hunt. Great food and drink. Super folks to meet and you can experience what the idiot Brits had to give up."

"I won't have to shoot anything, will I?" Sarah asked cautiously.

"No. We don't kill the foxes. The dogs corner 'em and scare the daylights out of them until we catch and release them for another day."

Mark looked for the thumbs up from Sarah and then said, "OK. Sounds interesting. Can you round us up the right riding gear?"

"I'm on it."

Sarah then added, "Mark, Foggy called me earlier to ask you to take the rest of the week off. He's planning a party for you at his cousin's place Friday night. I know Gorgarty's is one of your favorites. He said it would be mostly office folks, so no one from the embassy or NATO visitors should show up. That includes you, Tom. But we'll see you bright and early Saturday at Garristown for the fox hunting. Sound good?"

"Sounds great to me," Mark responded. "I'm planning on sleeping in my own bed for the next few nights. And it will probably be straight through the days as well."

The drive back in the limo was enjoyably comfortable, especially after all Mark had been through. Sitting with Sarah and holding hands was a great comfort and relief to them both.

"Thanks for the lift, Tom. Please let Sheldon know how much we appreciated it."

The driver dropped them at home and then took Tom back to the embassy, where he filled Pringle in on the little he could find out.

CHAPTER

22

Playing Golf

The next weeks passed very well for Jack Gobscheit and Sally Cartwright. Jack continued to be a celebrity of sorts and was to receive a medal from the prime minister as soon as his office could figure out which one was most appropriate. The US president had passed along to Sheldon Pringle that he would like to meet the now famous Mr. Gobscheit.

"We need an experienced negotiator with the guts to take on Putin head-to-head. We don't have anyone with his balls or his record of success. Maybe we could get him to Kyiv to help our team there."

"Mr. President, I know Jack Gobscheit and certainly agree with you. But, as you know, Ireland is a neutral country and is not involved with us in Ukraine."

"Well, damn it, they should be. The Irish here helped elect me and they damn well want this war over yesterday. Tell that to Gobscheit and his bosses. Is that a real name?"

"Yes, sir. It's been that as long as I've known him."

"Well, it doesn't sound very Irish to me. Tell him I called and pass along our appreciation for his tough negotiating skills. I want him on our team."

"Yes, sir, Mr. President. I will surely tell him that. We are planning to golf together tomorrow."

"Well, hold on now. At one of my clubs? I could fly over and join you both."

"Mr. President, we would hold up on our game until you can make the time to join us. But I'm unaware of any course that you own over here."

"Well, that may be, Pringle, I mean Sheldon, but you keep your tee-off time and let my secretary know. We'll see how fast this new Air Force One can fly. Maybe I'll tell the captain about an urgent meeting to test him. We spent a fortune on that damn plane. It's about the only one Boeing has made lately without parts falling off of it."

"I understand, sir. If for any reason you can't get here in time, we'll plan another occasion when you can."

"OK, Shelly. I'm planning on it. Oh, and one question for you. Does he cheat at golf?"

"Oh no, sir. He's an honest arrow."

They hung up and the ambassador ran to the bathroom.

***

And so, the coming weekend proved eventful. While the Jamisons and Tom Harrington were fox hunting, Ambassador Pringle and Jack Gobscheit teed off on schedule at 11:30 a.m. They had a third golfer with them who arrived at the last minute in a golf cart racing faster than anyone previously thought possible. Teams of American Secret Service agents were running hard to catch up.

"So this must be Mr. Gobscheit?"

"Yes, Mr. President, it's a great honor to introduce you both. Jack, our president very much wanted to meet you."

Gobscheit kept his composure and was very polite as the threesome teed off and were on their way for eighteen holes of golf. At the green approaching the second hole, the president was keen to get Gobscheit alone.

"So, Jack, I understand you and President Putin had some quality time together. He even had you down to his private dacha. That's a big honor for you, Jack. He must really like you. He and I really hit it off, too. Speaking of which, it's your turn. Maybe a five iron for this shot?"

As they approached the seventh hole, the president was feeling more comfortable with Jack.

"You know, Jack, you'll probably be seeing Vladimir or at least his people again. I think you have the makings of the next prime minister of Ireland. I really do. And I'll support you in any way I can. In fact, I'm going to talk to Shelly in a little while about an idea I have to speak to your parliament very soon. And I'll be sure to praise your remarkable negotiating skill and steadfast determination for success."

Jack Gobscheit could only express his appreciation as the threesome played on with Secret Service agents hiding in the bushes along the greens. By the green approaching the twelfth hole, the president recalled to Jack a little history of his relationship with Vladimir.

"You know, Jack, I have been discussing a hotel deal with him for years and even have a site ready to go in Moscow. I want you to help him along with this deal. It would mean a great deal to me and maybe you as well."

Jack was thunderstruck by it all, but kept his composure. "Yes, Mr. President, I will do my best for you. You can always count on me."

"I know I can, Jack. You know why? Because this is a neutral country and you folks don't bow down to any foreign leaders. Of course, if you ever do, I hope it will favor me."

When the threesome finished the final hole, the president said he had really enjoyed the game and was delighted with his score.

"Next time, Sheldon, I'll give you more of a handicap. Say, I have been thinking that while I'm over here, maybe you could arrange my making a presentation to the Irish parliament. I want to commend Jack here, but also share my thinking about these deep-sea communication cables and how important it all is."

"Well, sir, I'll see what I can do. Normally these things require a long lead time and the involvement of the Irish president."

"I was hoping for the day after tomorrow or Tuesday at the latest."

"Of course, I'll get my staff to work on this immediately. In the meanwhile, can I arrange a private meeting with the Irish president? Protocol is important."

"Sure, as long as he gets me in front of parliament by Tuesday."

CHAPTER

23

Back to School

Things were getting more eventful when Sarah returned to her school on Monday. Elena Markov was in a deep depression. When asked, she would only say that she had to fly to Moscow and that she had booked a flight leaving that evening. She apologized to the school for the short notice.

When Sarah pressed her for details, she said Sergay was in a coma in a Moscow hospital and that she needed to go to him right away.

"Oh my God, Elena. What in the world happened to him?"

"Sarah, our embassy seems confused. First, they said he drowned in the Black Sea. When I protested that he didn't swim and was fearful of deep water, they said he fell from an open window at his hotel. You know what this sounds like? We were so happy to be away from all that and posted here to Dublin." Elena burst into tears.

"I'm so sorry, dear Elena. If there is anything I can do, please let me know. Mark and I will send our prayers along with you for your husband's speedy recovery."

Elena spoke above her tears, while blowing her nose. "There is one thing. You know he was close with Jack Gobscheit, who's getting so much attention these days. Sergay was recalled to Moscow about the same time Mr. Gobscheit would have been heading there. I never heard from him since. Maybe I never will." She again burst into unconsolable crying.

CHAPTER

24

Parliament

The Irish president phoned Sheldon Pringle after having the American president to lunch on Monday.

"Your boss is a real gem, Sheldon. We had little to discuss and he was intent on talking about his golf game with you and Gobscheit. But even though parliament is out of session, I assured him we would reconvene on the occasion of his visit, which we so deeply appreciated, even on such short notice," he said mockingly.

"Are you listening to me, Ambassador Pringle? Or Shelly, as your boss refers to you. Did you know he says you cheated during your game on Sunday?"

"Mr. President, you have gone above and beyond the call of duty on this one. I assure you that we are all most grateful. I will plan to be at the session tomorrow, as will a number of our embassy staff. We have not seen a copy of the remarks he intends to give. So we will all anxiously await his comments."

"You mean his pontifications."

"Well, perhaps that, yes."

"Sheldon, you will owe me big time for this. You old golf cheat!"

"Yes, sir. I understand. We appreciate it more than I can express."

***

The following day, the US president was besieged by the Irish press and media outlets on the steps of parliament. He brushed past several ladies and gentlemen queuing up outside to greet him and introduce themselves. He seemed totally unaware that they were dignitaries from parliament and other embassies.

His speech was remarkable for many reasons. Tom Harrington and Mark Jamison were especially attentive to his comments about the undersea cable concerns and recent threats.

"You know, I love you Irish people. You're the finest people in the world. And you know why? Because you're neutral. Every country should be neutral. I celebrate countries that take care of their own concerns ahead of any others.

"You take the recent handling of the missing Russian device in your waters. I won't call it a nuclear device because we really don't know for sure what it was. I have doubts about my intelligence folks saying there were radiation indications. The point is, you handled it yourselves. You didn't call and whine to NATO. You picked your best man and sent him into the lion's den to reach an accord with the Russians. And you know, he was so tough and uncompromising that he was invited to negotiate directly with Putin. I like that. I respect that toughness and you should, too.

"Jack, get up here and stand beside me." Parliament rose to its feet and applauded Mr. Gobscheit as he walked to the dais.

"You know, you don't have anyone finer than this man, who stood face-to-face with Vladimir Putin. You know I call him Vladimir when we are together as we were several times and he showed great respect to me. Your man, Jack Gobscheit, served you well.

"You can sit back down now, Jack. Now about those cables. Who should safeguard those that come to your coasts? They are valuable to the whole world. Even my phone calls to Vladimir run through them. Well, I say neutral Ireland should be charged with protecting them. In fact, protecting and repairing them when necessary. I know you receive fees from the carriers that connect our countries. You should use some of that to equip submersibles that can check out the key lines and make sure they're in good repair. After all, who knows what the Russians were really doing down there? You know, they rely on them too. Like when Vladimir wants to call me.

"So congratulations to all of you for preserving your fabulous neutrality. Kudos to your man Jack Gobscheit. Geez, Jack, what a name. And special thanks to your president and his lovely wife for hosting me so graciously in your presidential palace yesterday. I love the Irish!"

Great applause filled the hall with a standing ovation. Jamison and Harrington looked sympathetically at each other, knowing their boss had just cut off the legs of Jamison's mission and both their commitments to NATO expansion.

CHAPTER

25

A New Minister of State for Defense

Over the next weeks, while the Irish president's staff worked on the most appropriate medal to award the distinguished Mr. Gobscheit, it became clear he would soon be replacing the existing minister and would move up to the post of Minister of State for Defense. After all, Irish talk shows and blogs seemed filled with Gobscheit, following the US president's laudatory comments before parliament.

Sensing this elevation would be forthcoming, NATO contacted the prime minister and requested a visit from Gobscheit to Brussels. NATO wanted to assure itself it could work with him and do a bit of vetting with the various member defense staffs. The prime minister was obliging and found a suitable conference that was coming up. NATO seemed always to be conducting conferences and meetings, so it was an easy matter to slip Jack Gobscheit into the mix. Besides, there was keen interest in Belgium to meet this legendary figure who could outmaneuver Putin face-to-face.

With Jack away, it was an easy matter to discuss the matter of his elevation to minister on his return, presuming all went well with his NATO vetting. Fogarty Gorgarty would be next up as deputy minister, a position for which he was extremely well qualified, as Jack's loyal number two for quite some time.

Well, as it turned out, Brussels was more than impressed with Jack. So much so that they decided to have him accompany some of their generals to Kyiv to meet with President Zelensky. They were convinced he could help teach Zelensky how to negotiate successfully with the murderous Russian president.

Gobscheit didn't disappoint and returned to Dublin with the gratitude of the Ukrainian government, in addition to the approving admiration of NATO. It appeared to all that Jack Gobscheit could do no wrong. The only problem with moving him up to defense minister was his popularity in parliament put him ahead of the prime minister himself. Now this was a problem, because the prime minister was not one to be shunted aside. Besides, he and the Irish president were very close and Gobscheit was a relative newcomer to these high echelons of Irish political power. And he had a reputation for cheating at golf.

And so, the prime minister needed to build a relationship with his defense minister's deputy,

Fogarty Gorgarty, to keep Gobscheit looking over his own shoulder and keeping his sights off higher office. Foggy was keen to help because he still had his doubts about Gobscheit.

So, when Jack Gobscheit was announced as the new defense minister, the public was delighted, but the prime minister and Foggy kept watchful and ever-suspecting eyes on him.

At about this time, three seemingly unrelated matters were unfolding. The Chinese were paying their respects to the new defense minister with a proposal. Elena Markov was successful in getting her husband removed to a hospital in Berlin. And Mark Jamison was asked to head to Germany and turn Markov to NATO's side if he showed signs of recovering.

Yes, and there was a fourth matter by the name of Abner Muscrat, who also came calling to the new defense minister shortly after he assumed his new office.

CHAPTER

26

The Chinese, the Americans,
and Abner Muscrat

There is a problem with neutrality. You need to be open and fair to all the world. Even to the Chinese, who really are friendless in the world despite everyone's efforts at cordiality, the Russians included.

The largest owner of undersea telecommunication cables is AT&T, with well over 200,000 miles of them. A close and closing second is China Telecom. Jack Gobscheit was fully read in on China's interests prior to their meeting with him. Australia had just rejected efforts of Huawei Marine Networks to bridge Brisbane and the Solomons, even though both wanted the link. But as we know, Jack sensed opportunity with everything he encountered. The aggressively expanding Digital Silk Road will have met its match with tough-as-nails Jack Gobscheit.

If the Chinese interest in getting a cable repair contract from Ireland could be sufficiently publicized, it would open up the need for getting such a contract from other interested parties, none of whom would be as unwelcome as the Chinese. So, he had his office masterfully issue a series of off-the-record leaks to the media that the Chinese wanted in, but Gobscheit was holding the line.

It was an easy task. The submarine cables to Taiwan's Matsu Islands had recently been cut by the PRC. The Taiwanese had publicized many other suspected cable disruptions, or "gray-zone aggression" as they characterized it. Then there was the fact that the Americans, through its Committee for the Assessment of Foreign Participation in the United States Telecommunications Services Sector (understandably known in shorthand as Team Telecom), had denied a submarine cable license for the Pacific Light Cable Network system to connect the USA with Hong Kong. The Americans cited that the repair and maintenance process would make the cables even more vulnerable to espionage from the Chinese Communist Party or other state actors.

Now the race was on for who would get more favorable treatment than the Chinese or its various entities. The next suitor would have been unexpected, except for a congratulatory phone call from the American president who said a close friend would be showing up. That friend was known to all the world as one of the biggest movers and shakers: Abner Muscrat.

Muscrat controlled major telecommunication links up in space and was now interested in seeing what he could do under the ocean. Of course, everyone fully realized that examining the cables meant the ability to eavesdrop on what was passing through them, just as the American NSA had been doing for years. Repairing also meant the ability to snip and replace damaged sections, which bestowed incredible opportunities for dire mischief in the wrong hands. This was one of the reasons why Ireland, with its pristine neutrality, was entrusted with the task of selecting the proper contractor for this purpose. And, as we know, Jack Gobscheit already had his preferences known only to himself.

Abner Muscrat made a strong case based on his successful record in other enterprises.

"Training large language models, along with data center computing and global storage, will take enormous distributed storage and hugely burden subsea traffic capacity," Muscrat pointed out. "No downtime can be permitted."

He went on to point out that Amazon, Google, Meta, and Microsoft now own or lease about half of all undersea bandwidth worldwide. Their rights allow them to lease bandwidth to others.

"These are private actors like me controlling what goes on down there. I just want to participate in securing what we all depend on," Mr. Muscrat added.

Despite the logic and eloquence of his arguments, Jack was sure the Irish parliament would hate the thought of one man collecting so much power. In short, Jack was sure he could destroy Muscrat's chances, much like the Chinese efforts that were doomed to failure. Each would make Jack look like the man holding fast the gates from all dangerous comers. And so, he had to explain to the Americans that their man would not be acceptable. There was little argument.

Next up came the US firm SubCom, the sole cable contractor for the US military. Gobscheit could anticipate strong lobbying by the USA and NATO in its favor. It gave another opportunity to leak these pressures to the media. In each case, the defense minister's representation of Irish concerns of neutrality would win the day and win him praise.

Jack realized that the procurement of the cable repair contract was an opportunity to acquire great wealth and power. All suitors wanted to leave gifts and curry favor. He always explained that the final decision would be parliament's, but his bank and investment accounts seemed to rise inexplicably. Sally Cartwright was in earthly heaven.

CHAPTER

27

Sergay Markov Awakens

With his new assignment, Mark was all over Sarah to pass on anything Elena Markov reported about the condition of her husband. Sarah and Elena had been playing online Scrabble and challenging each other with Wordle to pass the time for Elena, while she waited patiently in the German hospital. Mark was also in touch with the US ambassador in Berlin, who had assigned a political officer to monitor Markov's status and hopeful emergence from his coma.

The word came first from Elena to Sarah. Sergay opened his eyes and seemed to remember her, though he could not yet speak. That was enough for Mark to know the time had come. But since he hadn't met either of the Markovs, Jamison knew Sarah held the key and asked her to come along.

"What would you think about us visiting the Markovs? I mean Elena would appreciate it and you could say you were representing the concerns of the entire faculty and students of the Nord Anglia International School? I'm sure they could reassign your students for a week."

"Well, let me broach that with her first. I mean, she knows we are Americans. Maybe there are sensitivities?"

"Sensitivities? Based on what you told me, her only concern should be making sure we weren't coming from Moscow to finish the job on him."

"I get your point. I'll message her this evening and check with the school in the morning."

Mark also had to check with his new boss, Deputy Minister Gorgarty. Foggy was keen to learn as much as possible. Maybe something could be useful for the prime minister. If Foggy's suspicions were correct all along, there would be a lot to learn from Markov.

By the time the Jamisons reached the hospital, Markov had already been transferred to a safe facility run jointly by the Americans and Germans. A nurse was assigned there around the clock.

While the Jamisons were getting the details, Jack Gobscheit was also getting some information from the oligarch assigned to silence Markov. The oligarch was troubled to learn that Markov was flown to Germany, but couldn't believe it would matter because Markov seemed in such a hopeless condition. Still, the oligarch had his own contacts in Germany monitor him. Now the oligarch passed on the news to Gobscheit.

Jack Gobscheit was conflicted and torn. He truly liked Sergay, but he couldn't very well stand by to risk Markov revealing what he knew about the arrangements made with Putin. He had to get to Sergay Markov before he had a chance to open up about what he knew. But how? He tried to consider all the possibilities, but there were few.

It was possible, of course, that Sergay wouldn't remember anything after the coma, or that he would choose not to speak about it because of his own financial interest. But much depended on the "accident" that befell him and how much he would blame his Russian bosses and oligarch colleagues.

Jack was able to learn little in this regard and knew he had to come at it from another angle. What if he could become a hero to save Sergay from the clutches of the Russians and the Americans who now had him locked away in a German safe house? And if he could get Sergay painted as a NATO spy, anything he said would be discredited. Was there someone who could leverage relationships with Putin and with the US president to intervene, who could put Jack in a position to pull the strings and come out looking even better?

While all of Mr. Gobscheit's ruminations were swirling around in his highly adept and exceedingly devious brain, someone else was about to become privy to some remarkably secret information.

CHAPTER

28

In the Berlin Safe House

While in the safe house and before seeing Sergay Markov, Mark was separated from Sarah and taken into a special electronically insulated room, a Sensitive Compartmented Information Facility (SCIF), for questioning by the CIA station chief in Berlin. Not all safe houses had these, but Berlin had been a frequent locale for turning agents in the old Soviet days. Anything that leaked out meant certain death for someone thinking of becoming a double agent.

The station chief inquired about anything Jamison might have learned during his captivity on the trawler. Anything at all that Stavrov might have said about the nuclear device that was lost and whether they had found it.

Jamison said he attributed his release to the negotiations of Jack Gobscheit and presumed the Russians retrieved the device and departed with it.

"After all, that's what Gobscheit's positive publicity and celebrity was all about, wasn't it?" Mark asked.

"Well, yes and no," the station chief responded. She went on to congratulate Mark's navy colleagues who showed up first and retrieved it.

"Wait a minute. Then Gobscheit really didn't get the Russians to remove the device? All the hype is just that?"

"Well, he secured your release, that's for certain. And he probably is convinced he succeeded in his negotiation with Putin. Of course, that wouldn't have been so difficult if Putin suspected he no longer had it. It's easy to give up something you no longer have. Let's keep this between ourselves, of course, and let your Mr. Gobscheit continue to bask in his glories."

To Mark's questions about where the device was now, he was told only that: "Our side has it and is examining it."

"There is speculation that it may be made inert and replaced on the cable," the station chief continued. "Of course, that would break your guy's heart, but it could be used for leverage against the Russians. To show how sneaky they were to say it was removed when it wasn't."

Mark felt he was swimming in waters beyond his depth. Trying to process this new information, he stood silent.

The station chief said it was probably time to see what Mr. Markov did or didn't know. He thanked Mark for bringing his wife along to help with Elena's comfort level during the questioning. Before leaving their secure room, Mark asked about the doctor's report.

"Did it reveal what happened to him? Did he drown or did he fall out of a window?"

The station chief held back a smile. "I'm not sure where you got those ideas. He was poisoned. He was lucky to only be in a coma. The doctors here are experienced in the catalogue of concoctions Putin's friends come up with. Elena saved his life by getting him out of Moscow, that's for sure."

The station chief and Mark left the SCIF and joined Sarah. When the three entered Sergay Markov's room, they found him sitting up in bed and holding Elena's hand, with the nurse seated near his bedside. Sarah and Elena greeted each other warmly, and the husbands were introduced. The station chief was only identified as someone from the American embassy. The conversation was friendly and concentrated on Sergay's condition and the care he was receiving. He complained of continuing headaches, but that they were getting milder with the painkillers the nurse was administering. Everyone agreed that he looked good.

To the question of what he remembered happening to him, he said he didn't know. He thought he was having a heart attack and was pleased to awaken in a hospital bed in Moscow. He realized from Elena's presence there that he had been unconscious there for a number of days.

"Ten days," Elena clarified. "We were uncertain if he would pull out of it and the doctors there gave him little chance. That's when I arranged to get him here to Germany. Everyone knows the hospitals here are far superior to those in Russia, even those in Moscow. And of course, based on what I was told by our embassy in Dublin, I couldn't rule out foul play, though I certainly didn't want to say anything."

"What do you think about that, Sergay?" Mark inquired. "You know you are here for your safety in case anyone wanted to harm you there. Do you have any reason to believe anyone would want to injure or kill you? Could you tell us why you went back to Moscow? We are interested also in your relationship with Mr. Jack Gobscheit, Ireland's new defense minister and my boss."

"Gobscheit's your boss? I thought you were an American?" Sergay asked.

"Yes, to both. I was added to his staff because of my naval background and to be helpful with undersea cable issues. I understand you know Jack quite well."

"Yes, I translated for him during his meetings with President Putin. You must have heard about that?"

"Please tell us everything you can recall up until you felt you were having a heart attack."

Suddenly, Sergay Markov realized he held valuable information. Just like his friend Mr. Gobscheit, Sergay knew never to give away what could be sold.

"You know, my memory is really quite cloudy."

The station chief and Mark exchanged a glance that said Markov was going to be trouble.

CHAPTER

29

Markov and Muscrat

Jack Gobscheit couldn't sleep thinking about what Sergay Markov might say with the Americans questioning him in a Berlin safe house. There had to be a way to come out of this, no matter what he might say. Jack was confident that Sergay was no fool, but doubts lingered.

So Jack wanted to be sure and maybe launch a plan that could help them both. In the back of his mind was someone he had recently met and who could unknowingly be of assistance. He felt this fellow would do anything to increase his global power and the prospect of monitoring the cables would be a great prize for him. Abner Muscrat was still in Europe and a call to an assistant brought him back to Dublin the next day.

Jack explained things to Abner in deepest confidence. He explained that Ireland's ability to procure the cable repair contracts was only because of its neutrality and the American president's full support of its project. He told Muscrat that there were other forces at play that would do anything to take control of the contract. These same forces, Jack told Abner, would do anything to force Ireland to surrender its precious neutrality and join NATO.

"We can never let that happen!" blurted Abner Muscrat.

Jack was so pleased to hear this and continued with his confidential briefing, telling Muscrat that the Russians were on the same page and one of their top people may be in trouble.

"How can I help?" exclaimed Abner, again to Jack's great satisfaction.

"This Russian fellow may be forced to turn his loyalty in favor of NATO and could say anything they put in his mouth. He is actually an old friend and he may be placed in a compromised situation."

"So what do you want me to do?"

"Abner, here's the thing. The fellow is named Sergay Markov and he is currently with his wife in Berlin. I have reason to believe he is being held illegally by the Americans there. He can't go back to the Russians after his interrogation there. They would never trust him." Jack was careful to conceal they previously tried to murder Markov and that's why he was in the safe house to begin with. "We can't very well let the Americans and NATO have him, can we?"

"Of course not."

"So, Abner, what would you think about hiring Sergay and bringing him aboard your staff,

119

or in any suitable position? He is a brilliant fellow with a great command of languages and knows his way around. If you were to notify your connections in Washington and Berlin and let them know one of your folks is being unlawfully detained, I'm sure it would resolve the situation immediately. And Sergay could be very useful to you in your bidding for the cable repair contracts."

"I understand the situation fully, Jack. I'll call my folks in Germany to jump on this. Our president if necessary. Markov now works for Muscrat!"

They parted with a warm handshake and Jack immediately felt a huge sense of relief.

C H A P T E R

30

Confusion in Berlin

When Sergay Markov started to complain about his head hurting, the Jamisons and the station chief stepped outside his room to be read an urgent message from German intelligence. The Germans were ordering the Markovs immediate release into the care of Abner Muscrat, who was now Markov's employer. They were to transport the Markovs to the German foreign ministry, where they would be picked up by Muscrat's local representatives. Jamison was astonished.

First his efforts to get Ireland into NATO were dashed by the US president, and now his assignment to work on Markov was undercut by that president's close friend and supporter, Abner Muscrat. Jamison looked to Sarah for comfort.

"Listen, Mark, it's not all bad news. I mean, we're in Berlin and you don't need to be back in the office for a few days. Remember the fun we used to have over here. Let's not be in a hurry to get back," Sarah said wistfully.

Sarah was referring to the time when they lived in a castle in Salzburg and traveled extensively in Germany, while Mark raised funds and support for his think tank there. In those days, Bonn was still the capital of West Germany and demonstrations were in full progress, leading to the Berlin Wall coming down.

"Just one night, I'm afraid," Mark responded. "Foggy needs me to explain all this, and I'll need to clue in Tom Harrington. Something tells me Gobscheit already knows everything and probably had a hand in it. This is all going a little too smoothly for him."

When the Markovs were picked up at the German foreign ministry, they were both brimming with questions. Muscrat's representative told them to hold off until Abner Muscrat personally met with them at Berlin's Rocco Forte Hotel de Rome, where they were now headed. They pulled up to Bebelplatz and to the former nineteenth-century bank building, which had been elegantly restored and modernized. The driver told Sergay that since he was now an important figure in the Muscrat organization, a suite had been arranged and they were to rest up until Mr. Muscrat called on them later in the evening. Dinner would be arranged and sent up to their suite. Sergay and Elena just stared at each other, not having a clue what to expect.

"Any enemies you might have can't get to us here," Elena told Sergay as she phoned down to order a bottle of the hotel's finest vodka and caviar. They both needed a drink.

"Do I have enemies?" Sergay asked innocently.

"When you met with Putin, were others there besides Jack Gobscheit?"

"Only in the afternoon meeting. A number of the oligarchs who hang onto the president were there. We were told we would all be business partners."

"And how does Abner Muscrat fit into all this?"

"I really have no idea."

The knock on their door was expected to be the libation they ordered and badly needed. Instead, it was a German gentleman with an attaché case. He said he was sent by Mr. Muscrat with some documents for Mr. Markov to go over and sign. It was important that they were signed on this date to establish the veracity of what Mr. Muskrat had earlier announced.

As the Markovs looked through the papers and saw the extremely generous compensation involved, there was another knock on the door with the vodka and caviar.

They looked at the gentleman with the briefcase and asked if all this was genuine. They were told Mr. Markov would be receiving a cashier's check immediately upon signing.

"You mean right now?" Sergay asked.

The gentleman handed the pen from his coat pocket to Sergay and said the check was already made out for 100,000 US dollars. The Markovs looked at each other. Sergay took the pen, and while Elena poured the vodka, the deal was done with a toast to the gentleman and to Mr. Muscrat, whom neither had met.

CHAPTER

31

Irish Undersea Security Services

When the Markovs returned to Dublin, Sergay was a director of a new company created specifically to examine and repair damaged undersea cables. It was a subsidiary of a larger company concerned with oil and natural gas pipelines, including those of Russia's Rosncft and Gazprom, British Petroleum, Shell, and Exxon Mobile. It had investors from around the world. Muscrat protected his investment with Markov's appointment that was approved by the remainder of its board of directors.

Not unexpectedly, the undersea cable security bid of the Irish Undersea Security Services (IUSS) soon had the support of the defense minister and was awaiting approval by the prime minister. The PM did not care for the media blitz designed to gain the support of parliament before his own decision could be reached. Nor, despite his suspicions, could he prove that Defense Minister Gobscheit was behind it. Approval would keep the

Chinese out, as well as the Americans, NATO, and the Russians. It would give an Irish company a leg up and support jobs as it built its infrastructure, repair ships, and submersibles.

Fogarty Gorgarty was keenly aware of his suspicions of the linkage between Gobscheit and Markov. Now they were sufficient for him to alert NATO and raise them with the PM. Jamison had failed to get Markov to disclose what really went on in Moscow, in spite of his near-death exit. He must have learned too much or been involved too closely in what Putin or his henchmen wanted to achieve. Markov told Jamison he was there to translate for Gobscheit. And now Markov showed up working for Abner Muscrat and heading the IUSS. Foggy's suspicions were overflowing and Jamison was fully on board with him.

Jamison worked into the night with Tom Harrington and Sheldon Pringle at the US embassy. Their posture was to get Subsea, the US contractor for cable repair, to be promoted in parliament and to build enough support there to back the PM. They knew that any mention of Subsea would raise the hackles of the Greens and others opposed to increased NATO involvement.

But their strategy would force Gobscheit's hand and test the level of his support and how far he was willing to go to get the IUSS the contract award. Then there was the issue of Muscrat and his friendship with both the American and Russian presidents. Muscrat had a big stake in IUSS and appeared determined to control as much digital telecommunication as possible in both space and undersea domains.

Jamison, Harrington, and Pringle worked late into the night trying to figure out the parliamentary lineup to see if there might be enough support to then take the proposal to the PM. They knew Foggy would be the right person to approach the PM.

Parliament wouldn't take up the matter without hearing from the PM, but the media continued to clamor for the IUSS and finding support for Subsea was difficult. The PM was receptive to Foggy and really wanted to deliver a setback to Mr. Gobscheit, whom he rightly perceived was after his job. He determined the media leaks favoring IUSS were clearly coming from Gobscheit's staff and he had to be putting them up to it. But how to cripple his own very popular defense minister?

***

In the following days, Mark Jamison launched a plan. His knowledge of how the Nord Stream 2 pipeline was sabotaged gave him great respect for the talents of American Navy divers. He also received some very sensitive information while at the safe house in Berlin. But this plan would need to be so carefully guarded he couldn't discuss it even with Harrington or Pringle. He needed to get back to visit ONI and, if he could get the admiral on board, have her carry the idea up to the Pentagon and White House.

CHAPTER

32

Back to Suitland

Jamison's call to the admiral from Dublin got him aboard the next flight heading to the Baltimore Washington International Airport and an awaiting helicopter on the tarmac. Within minutes, he was en route to a landing pad on the grounds of the Naval Intelligence offices at Suitland, Maryland. They met at her offices and proceeded directly to the SCIF.

He described the importance of the contract award that could go to the IUSS. She immediately indicated she was already fully briefed on the matter by Captain Tom Harrington, with whom she had just spoken on a secure line. When she asked Jamison why his matter couldn't also have been shared in this fashion, he reminded her that her phone conversation, even though scrambled, likely came over the very undersea cables that they wanted to protect. She, certainly more than most, would appreciate the sophisticated AI-driven decoding that could take place through cable taps and monitoring.

Jamison stressed that surveillance to check the cables for any damage and to make repairs carries with it great risks of monitoring the communications and the ability to sever them.

"I can't tell you for certain that the Irish defense minister and the IUSS are connected in some way. But we suspect that connection began with the Russian embassy in Dublin and continued to Moscow, through the efforts of Jack Gobscheit's friend Sergay Markov. Markov is today a director of the company, representing the interests of his employer, Abner Muscrat."

"And we know the Russian involvement within the company, including some oligarchs close to Putin," the admiral added. "And Muscrat? Well, even this facility doesn't feel secure enough for me to tell you what we have on this guy. But, of course, he's close to the president."

"He even campaigned for him," Jamison added.

"Don't remind me. I get it. So what's your plan?"

Jamison told her of his conversation in the safe house SCIF with the CIA station chief in Berlin.

"If it was accurate," he related, "our navy very well may have picked up the lost Russian nuke in Irish waters. Gobscheit's celebrity came when he negotiated its removal. But what if it wasn't removed?"

"You're saying that Gobscheit and Putin could both be made to look like fools..."

"Yes, if we replace the device. Maybe with enough radiation to copy the signature but without the explosive capability," Jamison finished her thought and his idea.

"And what if a NATO exercise involving Subsea discovered it and Subsea alerted the Irish defense minister. That would really put your Mr. Gobscheit in an awkward position, wouldn't it?" the admiral suggested.

"And if he didn't disclose it, we leak the information directly to the Irish prime minister and parliament. Mr. Gorgarty is perfect to do this and he's itching to do it!" Jamison added.

"Well, Captain, it looks like we need to confirm whether we picked up the device and whether it can be modified as you suggest. Then whether we can get it back in place and schedule an exercise involving our contractor Subsea. All that will take some time, so you folks try your best to hold up parliamentary discussions on the subject."

"We'll try our best. Thanks for this meeting on short notice."

Jamison's plan seemed to be launched.

With a few hours to fill before his return flight, he decided to call on an old colleague still working at the nearby Washington Naval Yard. In his working days there, the Yard was known to sit astride a tough neighborhood outside its walled and castle-like entry portal. Starting like clockwork at six in the evening, police sirens could be heard that lasted through most of the night. It was not far from here, at the base of the Anacostia Bridge, that one of Mark and Sarah's closest personal friends was murdered.

The Chief of Naval Operations formerly occupied the finest house and grounds at the Naval Observatory, off Massachusetts Avenue in the District's Northwest. Then Vice President Walter Mondale took the quarters for his own and relegated the Navy Chief to living with the nocturnal sirens in this part of the District's Southeast. At the time, President Jimmy Carter was a Naval Academy graduate who apparently was not keen to respect that honored housing tradition.

The old colleague Mark went to see had kept a file on Abner Muscrat.

CHAPTER

33

The Muscrat File

The file Jamison retrieved from his old colleague at the Washington Navy Yard revealed a great deal and made interesting reading on his flight back to Dublin.

In essence, Abner Muscrat's overarching goal was to shape a future where humanity is sustainable, technologically advanced, and resilient. He was driven by a desire to push the boundaries of innovation and make a positive impact on the world. However, to accomplish this, he needed to eliminate resistance from popular culture and democratic norms. His acquisition of a major content provider and entry into political relationships was to this end. He realized that control of global data transmission furthered this agenda while also being incredibly lucrative. Fees from the use of his linked satellite constellation were funding his larger space exploration projects.

The analysis Jamison was reading said Muscrat would seek to dominate global connectivity and this would lead inexorably to direct involvement in the global data infrastructure, including undersea cables that were critical for high-bandwidth, low-latency applications.

The analysts saw great promise from Muscrat's global operations and connections at the highest levels of government and multinational business. This included the potential to bridge geopolitical rivalries and deter or end conflicts that were counterproductive to his agenda and globalization interests generally. Along with this promise, however, came a great challenge of compatibility with democratic norms.

CHAPTER

34

The Kremlin

The lights stayed on in the Russian Federation president's offices. The lost nuclear device was an embarrassment. It's true that the Irish celebrated their negotiation of its removal, but in reality, it was neither retrieved nor removed by the Russians, or, very possibly, by anyone else. There was a slight chance that Irish divers may have located it, but the network of Russian agents across Ireland reported nothing of the kind. There were other possibilities that were keeping Putin's folks awake. NATO must be trying to get hold of it, or, even worse, could they already have it?

With these concerns, the decision was reached to conduct a naval exercise that would disguise the hunt for their lost device. And to help the chances of actually locating it, while promoting the company Putin and Muscrat controlled, they would include the IUSS.

So, within weeks, Ireland was protesting the announced plans of both NATO and the Russian Federation to hold naval exercises that would encroach within its waters. The Russians felt sure that the NATO exercise was also to hunt for Russia's nuclear device. The Russians had to find it first. Of course, the NATO exercise wasn't just to find it, it was to plant it right back where the American submarine had found it, then to announce locating it to the Irish.

The announced naval exercises also had the salutary effect of so enraging parliament that it occupied nearly all its discussions. The procurement of cable repair services was temporarily off the table. Minister Gobscheit was not pleased.

CHAPTER

35

The Irish Parliament

Mark Jamison had no real breakthroughs in his efforts to persuade members of the Irish parliament to favor joining NATO. Neutrality was just seen as being too fundamental to a people that relished every aspect of their independence. This was probably natural after so many years of subservience to the British crown. Perhaps it was just part of Irish pride in its rich culture.

Ireland's Green Party remained staunchly committed to the country's policy of military neutrality. They were opposed to Ireland joining NATO or participating in any military alliances. The party considered Ireland's neutrality to be a cornerstone of its foreign policy. Neutrality, it was felt, allowed the country to play a more constructive role in international affairs through diplomacy and humanitarian aid. The Green Party consistently advocated for a peaceful and nonviolent approach to international relations and was critical of any actions that could undermine Ireland's neutral status. Jamison respected the Greens and every aspect of their agenda, but he had an assignment to carry out and needed to see it through.

Jamison saw more hope with the Fianna Fáil party, though it, too, had historically been a strong advocate for Irish neutrality. In recent years, he learned there was a growing debate within the party about Ireland's role in European security. Still, he could find no real opening for his powers of persuasion.

Similarly, there were glimmers with Sinn Féin, though it, too, was traditionally a strong supporter of Irish neutrality. However, as the party grew in popularity, there was some internal debate about whether Ireland should play a more active role in international affairs.

The parties more open to closer ties with NATO included Fine Gael. The party supported Ireland's participation in NATO's Partnership for Peace program and advocated for a stronger Irish role in European security.

The Labour Party showed more openness to closer cooperation with NATO. It supported Ireland's participation in EU-led peacekeeping missions and called for a more robust Irish defense policy. This was still not signing on with NATO, however.

While these efforts gained little real traction, something held greater promise. All representatives of the various parties came together in total agreement on one matter. Naval exercises in Irish waters by either the Russian Federation or NATO were vehemently opposed. In fact, some were calling it an act of aggression, no matter the notification. They wanted the government to explain what the Irish forces were prepared to do about it. The prime minister said the defense minister would never permit it.

In private discussions with the PM, Gobscheit expressed the matter differently, however. He indicated that allowing both exercises would be consistent with Irish neutrality by not showing partiality. Fogarty was asked his opinion, which gave him the opportunity to share the discussion with Jamison.

Jamison immediately saw an opening. If he got word that the device was back in place, he would recommend the NATO exercise be canceled to placate Ireland's concerns. This would leave the Russians looking like an aggressor. And if NATO intelligence were then leaked that Putin had not removed the device after all, Mr. Gobscheit would be hard pressed for an explanation.

Besides, the NATO exercise was really unnecessary to leaking the story. How NATO learned the device was still there could be labeled as highly classified to keep the public and the Russians guessing.

Jamison set about working his plan with Tom Harrington, who headed immediately to Brussels.

Harrington and Jamison coordinated closely and worked the plan from both Dublin and NATO headquarters.

So the tension mounted until Jamison received word that the navy divers from the American submarine were successful. What happened next was an astonishing series of events.

Even before the NATO ships changed course, Gobscheit received an urgent call from Markov that NATO was canceling its exercise. How did he learn it even before the defense minister? Markov said the optics could be disastrous. The Russians couldn't call off their exercise because they needed to locate and account for their nuclear device. Gobscheit and Markov were in full agreement that the only way to keep the Russians from looking like an aggressor would be keeping the NATO exercise going. But how?

Gobscheit's secure line was lit up with calls to Abner Muscrat to reach out to the American president. The defense minister even jumped outside protocol to initiate a call to the White House, asking for a call back from the US president.

Within ten minutes, the American president was on the line, calling Jack by his first name and speaking in a friendly and cordial manner that gave him great hope of assistance. The president recalled their golf game in detail and asked for any progress on the hotel favor he requested.

Mr. Gobscheit felt obliged to change the subject to ask if he was aware of the scheduled naval exercises by the Russian Federation and by NATO in Irish waters. The president said he just got off the phone with Abner Muscrat who mentioned something about it. He told Jack that it looked to him that he was being asked for a favor. The US president then asked Jack what would be in it for his reelection or for the hotel deal he desired?

Gobscheit said the commitment to Irish neutrality would be furthered with NATO continuing its planned naval exercise. Without it, Russia would look aggressive, which would bolster support for NATO in the Irish parliament. Rather than responding to Jack's plea, the president asked if Jack would speak with Putin on his behalf about the hotel deal he wanted in Moscow. All Jack could say was he would try his best, but getting the NATO ships to proceed was an urgent matter.

"You know, Jack, they are all urgent matters," the president responded. "You bring me some positive news about my requests and I'll see what I can do. I know I can count on you, Jack. You have a way with Vladimir Vladimirovich, after all."

For the first time, Jack Gobscheit felt a gnawing sensation deep within his anatomy.

***

The following day, parliament received a briefing from Jack Gobscheit and was none too pleased. He tried to take credit for NATO turning its ships around, but the northern fleet of the Russian Federation was entering Irish waters.

Parliament asked about his tough negotiating skills with Putin and why he hadn't been successful in also turning the Russian ships around. Unlike his reputation, this time he had no answer. He feared for what could unravel.

CHAPTER

36

Jamison's Opportunity

With the snare for Gobscheit in place, Jamison set to work with Harrington to have NATO leak a startling development. NATO sensors detected that the Russian device appeared to be in place still. The logical conclusion was that it had never been removed despite Putin's solemn promise. The media jumped on the story.

Rather than being a hero, it now seemed that Jack Gobscheit, and through him all Ireland, had been duped. Adding to the perfidy, the Russian northern naval fleet was now steaming freely and unopposed off Irish shores. Jack Gobscheit's star had plummeted and was now as underwater as the device the Russians were searching for.

Jamison and Harrington were not through, however. While the defense minister was being grilled in parliament, it was learned that the AE6 cable had gone dead. Efforts to reroute all telecommunications were occurring automatically.

But then, one by one, other cables were going down and the remaining lines were overloaded and unavailable for rerouting. At their request, the prime minister and parliament were being kept fully apprised.

Calls to the PM were coming in from the high-tech hub in Dublin and from County Cork's technology parks. Apple's European CEO in Hollyhill and its overall CEO in Sunnyvale were both on the phone with the PM, as were corporate representatives from Dublin's South County Business Park at Carmanhall and Leopardstown.

The emergency session of parliament continued late into the night with backup generators supplying the power, since the entire fiber-optic-controlled grid had shut down.

There were those who said Ireland's decision to join NATO was literally made in the dark.

It had become clear to everyone that Ireland's high-tech present and future was linked by undersea cables. The rest of Europe depended on Ireland's sending and receiving base stations. Staying neutral after the invasion of Ukraine and the bombing of the Nord Stream 2 pipelines may not have been fully realistic. In any event, Jamison felt he was just giving a push to move the inevitable along. He was fulfilling his mission.

CHAPTER

37

Neutral No More

The swiftness of events led to a full inquiry into Jack Gobscheit's ill-fated trip to Moscow and what may or may not have been concluded there. While investigations were underway, the prime minister reassigned him according to an earlier promise. He went to Fisheries.

Fogarty Gorgarty was elevated to defense minister, to the delight of Brussels.

The cable cutoffs lasted only until the Irish parliament voted in favor of accession. Remarkably, no cables were cut or even damaged. There had been a mysterious jamming of the signals in the affected fiber-optic cables that incapacitated them. It was a remarkable coincidence that NATO had been testing just such a technique to interfere with Russia's and China's telecommunications.

"It is basically just overloading the circuits to shut them down," Captain Harrington had related to Captain Jamison.

NATO learned that if a jamming action is aimed at paralyzing a central node, for example, a base station, an access point, or a gateway, this can lead to a collapse of the entire network. This is called a denial-of-service (DoS) attack that intentionally causes interference over the range of acoustic frequencies used by legitimate underwater network nodes.

NATO members swiftly voted unanimously to approve Ireland's application for accession.

The Markovs were reassigned by Muscrat to Cyprus, where Sergay worked on undersea cable and pipeline security. Despite the earlier efforts of a certain oligarch to terminate his hotel and casino interests, Markov was receiving periodic installments in his numbered account there.

Among his most welcomed visitors to the shoreside cafés at Larnica, was his old friend Jack Gobscheit, who would take time away from his duties at fisheries to make periodic withdrawals from his Cypriot bank account there. The two were not infrequently seen at the casinos of various properties in which they shared financial interests. Elena and Sally also enjoyed each other's companionship in their favorite pastime of shopping.

The Jamisons stayed on a little longer in Dublin. Mark continued to work with Foggy, who, knowing Mark's legal background, assigned him the task of sorting out what laws applied to the protection of undersea cables. Harrington approved the extension because the embassy was in the dark on the subject. The truth was that so was everyone else. The oceans are pretty lawless places and the confusion stems from nearly two centuries of neglect.

Foggy soon received a report summarizing the serious danger that exists from malicious attacks not only to interrupt connectivity but also to tap into the cables and eavesdrop. Despite this, in international waters it is the laws of the perpetrator's state, not the state that owns the cable that determines liability. The international community has yet to take undersea cable security seriously. There are no internationally recognized protocols to deter actions against undersea cables and prioritize the security of digital communications. Neither the UN nor the International Telecommunication Union (ITU) has acted to remedy this.

The situation becomes amazingly complex with the realization that there are competing multinational companies operating in this space, while international accords only deal with nations, that is: state actors. Competing nonstate actors, whether armed groups or large multinational business companies, could also interfere with the cables. The largest cable owners are AT&T, China Telecom, Facebook, Google, and Amazon.

Facebook and Google are jointly building Apricot, which will connect East Asia and the USA. A Facebook-led consortium called 2Africa will connect thirty-three African nations, and become the longest single telecommunications cable extending approximately 30,000 miles.

CHAPTER

38

Complexity, Neutrality, and Democracy

As the Jamisons were packing to return from Dublin to Angel Landing, there was still time for a final fox hunt with Tom Harrington and Seamus McGrath. At a picnic lunch together with the horses tethered to the birch trees nearby, a lively discussion turned to many things, carried along with the very independent spirit of Seamus and his love of all things Irish. Above all was his love of freedom and his concerns for Ireland joining NATO. It troubled him greatly. Mark and Tom had to remain silent, though they were in full personal agreement.

"It was those damned undersea cables," McGrath lamented. "I would have preferred we give up all the high-tech stuff and just rely on ourselves. Look around at the land here. There is everything anyone could ask for. We can grow anything in this fertile soil. The foxes love it here." He smiled.

In spite of these shared yearnings for freedom, they all agreed that the world had become so complex and interconnected that the longing to "breathe free" had really become increasingly impossible. The damned cables really captured the dilemma. First of all, they were entirely out of sight and hidden. Most hitherto had no idea of their existence, let alone their importance. Governments really didn't control them as much as exploit them. Snowden had revealed as much with the NSA's tapping into them. Recent evidence also pointed to Russia and China. Mark's research showed scant interest of major countries to create legally enforceable rules governing them.

Then there was the issue of ownership. The cables were a matter of private business interests, not governments, in spite of their becoming essential to the very continuing existence of those governments. The power of any cable owner was enormous. AT&T chose to cooperate with the NSA. It wasn't forced to collaborate. The collective power of the cable owners would be unimaginable.

The conversation went to Abner Muscrat, one of the most powerful individuals on the planet. He possessed significant control of satellite communications and even space exploration, as the exclusive role of governments was rapidly receding. He was an American citizen, but through his business holdings, was really even more than an international figure. He became a nonstate actor, free to deal with heads of state of any and every nation and to negotiate freely with them. His wealth and prestige even swayed elections in countries still claiming to be democracies. But was there really any such thing as true democracies in the age of interconnected multinational corporations?

Seamus brought the discussion back to Ireland. If there were still a viable democracy on the planet, he posited, it would be Ireland's. The wide-ranging and unconstrained discussions in the Irish parliament seemed to attest to his pronouncement.

Sarah, Mark, and Tom could only nod their heads in silent agreement. Mark felt bold enough to point out how it seemed America's two political parties offered less and less real choice to voters. Sarah brought up the matter of corruption of their accepting unlimited funds from major donors disguised through contrived intermediaries, the so-called Political Action Committees or PACS.

"Under the US Supreme Court decision in Citizens United," she said, "corporations are given the full latitude of private citizens. The parties solicit and accept huge corporate contributions, which sets the real agenda. What is disclosed to the public may be entirely different."

"Yep, we're far from perfect. But we're still trying to make things better for the world," added Tom.

"I hope you're right, Tom," responded Mark. "I try hard sometimes to believe that."

"I mean, do we really have a democracy anymore?" added Sarah. "I read an interesting proposal to break the influence of a largely bought and paid-for Congress. Why not select citizens at random to serve for a limited time, much like jury duty?"

"You know, we may be way ahead of you on this," responded Seamus. "In 2016, our Irish parliament established the first Ireland Citizens' Assembly. This involves ninety-nine randomly selected citizens, chaired by a Supreme Court judge, who meet over several weekends to discuss the most controversial issues in the country."

The Ireland Citizens' Assembly Seamus referred to began with the issue of abortion. They heard from medical, legal, and ethical experts, debated options, and by nearly a two-thirds majority, recommended repealing the country's abortion ban. This citizen body, ninety-nine strangers thrown together, helped resolve a long-standing political stalemate in the country and cleared the way for a 2018 national referendum that legalized abortion. Since then, Irish Citizens' Assemblies have convened to consider drug policy, gender equality, and other topics.

As the four of them finished with their picnic lunch and went to gather the horses, Seamus raised another matter. "I've heard that political correctness is tying you folks in knots over there, just as it did to the English. Many of the folks riding with us today came over from England for the weekend. You know, you folks and the Brits supply weapons killing innocent folks every day. Do you suppose their consciences are eased by sparing their foxes from being scared by dogs?"

As he said that, his German Pointer Otto was wagging its tail and telling all of them to mount up.

CHAPTER

39

Regrets

The Jamison farewell party was hosted by Defense Minister Gorgarty. Many from the office were despondent over Ireland's surrender of its neutrality by joining NATO. Neither Mark nor Foggy could breathe a word about their role. As Mark got more inebriated, he started to agree with the sentiment. It was a one-way ticket to a less independent and democratic future. Mark knew he and Foggy were helping to safeguard Ireland's security by what they had helped achieve, but at what price? There was no going back. The world had become more dangerous after Russia's invasion of Ukraine and sides had to be taken. Mark and Foggy only helped Ireland make the inevitable decision and did so while there was still time.

Those thoughts helped, but were countered by the Irish ballads and sentimental tunes of glory and suffering in the long years seeking independence from domination. And wouldn't membership in NATO bring another form of domination from outside its borders? Brussels was already asking for things and reminding Dublin of its commitments to European security.

But security from whom, from what? Did NATO offer security from the multinationals that were increasingly running the show and operating on both sides of any dispute or controversy? What security would NATO offer in a world where artificial intelligence added incredible new power to the multinationals that were already collecting massive amounts of data and transmitting it across the cables they controlled?

What chance did the Ireland Citizens' Assembly have to compete with what would be requested and demanded from outside Ireland's borders? Mark knew the inevitable tension between freedom and independence on the one hand, and security on the other. Enough emphasis on the latter and the former is eroded until it disappears. All that's left are weaponized bunkers protecting conforming populations gathered together in mutual mistrust of those outside their shelter.

The Irish whiskey, and songs of lament and sorrow, were taking a toll on Mark's self-esteem for accomplishing his mission.

He approached Foggy and stared into his dazzling, mismatched eyes.

"What have we done, Foggy?"

"Mark, you have achieved your goals and the mission. That's all you should be concerned with.

Go back home and feel you have scored another success in your illustrious career."

"Foggy, you're the defense minister of this great country. I want you to protect it not only from outside threats. I want you to protect the heart of this nation, its culture and values and its openness to all comers. Just because you are in NATO now, doesn't mean any of this has to be surrendered. Please fight against what may be facing us all, especially as technology and AI move us along faster than we have time to think."

With that, Mark raised his glass in a toast to Foggy and to all near enough to hear him. "I drink to the Irish people. May you survive every storm and obstacle in your path and find the right way to live in this world for all of us."

CHAPTER

40

Home Again

It was nearly a year to the day when Mark and Sarah returned home to Angel Landing. Everything was as they left it. Many didn't even realize they had been away.

Their friend Bjorn Ingman was the first to have a small welcoming gathering on the expansive wooden deck of his home. The view of the bay with San Francisco sitting proudly above the opposite shore and boats with white billowing sails was still magnificent. The weather was noticeably better than Ireland's.

"So I see Ireland's now in NATO," was among Bjorn's first comments. "You have anything to do with that?"

"Not a thing, but it's sure an interesting development, isn't it?" Mark answered.

"You know, Jamison, I got pretty excited when Sweden and Norway joined up. But you weren't there, were you?"

"Nope, but I wish I had been. Why?"

"Just asking," Ingman replied, with something like a Cheshire cat look on his face.

"OK, out with it, Bjorn."

"Well, Dublin is seeing some of its largest protests ever recorded. When Ireland refused a British airbase on its soil, I knew things would start to unravel. Defense in depth, the Brits called it. I can imagine what many Irish called it."

"Yes, I'm reading about all this."

"Then they didn't react well when our president called them idiots for signing on."

"I read that also. That was when the Irish learned that spending 2 percent of their GDP for defense would decimate many of the domestic programs they hold dear. And at least 20 percent of that is required for major new equipment purchases. There is no defense industry in Ireland making that equipment. So those funds go immediately out of the country."

Jamison continued, "Of course, the comments of our president were like pouring gasoline on an open wound. That's a bad analogy certainly, but you understand," while avoiding direct eye contact with Ingman. He aimed to reveal nothing at all in his expression. He was finding it hard, however, to come up with the right words, especially in responding to such a close friend and astute interrogator.

"You think they'll stay in?"

"You mean in NATO? Well, no member has ever left. They all have a right to though, with a year's notice to our president."

"Jamison, you just came back from over there. You must know these people to some extent. So I'm asking you for your opinion. Do you think they'll stay in?"

"It really depends on the threat they perceive in this changing world. If it's from the Russians, they may stay onboard. But think about the threats all countries are facing today. If it's climate change, spending 2 percent of GDP on weapons doesn't really make sense, does it? The same would be true with confronting the next pandemic. What if the real threat is coming from the huge multinationals that seem to be buying up everything and telling people what to think and certainly what to buy."

"I'm following you. Can I get you another drink?"

"Sure, in just a minute. But let me finish the thought. Companies like Google and Amazon, and certainly big oil and oil service companies, operate everywhere in complex webs of legal relationships that go outside of efforts to control or contain them. They never really left Russia or China and are burrowing in everywhere. Even Facebook, or Meta Platforms as it prefers being called, is linked up globally, and it's now owning the links that others use and depend on. Couple that with the data centers, all linked up around the world. People are saving everything to the cloud without realizing where their data is going and how it's getting there. These connections and storage 'clouds' all look to be owned and controlled by these multinationals."

"Now *I* need another drink," Ingman said, stepping away from Mark.

CHAPTER

41

Updates from Tom Harrington

Mark continued to be in touch with Tom Harrington, seeking updates over his nonsecure phone. Calling Foggy would put him at risk while all Irish eyes and ears were focused on Ireland's new relationship with NATO.

Tom told him that the Ireland Citizens' Assembly had convened to discuss whether Ireland should remain in NATO. The second thoughts many in parliament were having reminded Tom of the British vote to leave the European Union. Many who voted in its referendum for Brexit were asking the next day what Brexit was. Parliament wanted to shed some of the heat for its precipitous decision onto the Assembly, now taking it up. The media were referring to Ireland's decision to join NATO as the decision made in the dark that now required more thoughtful reconsideration.

Tom told Mark that, by coincidence, their friend Seamus McGrath had been selected for membership on the Assembly and was now in conferences of its ninety-nine members, all selected at random. It was not unlike jury duty, but instead of deciding the fate of individuals, this concerned the fate of their entire nation.

Seamus, by Tom's account, was taking his role very seriously and would disclose nothing of its deliberations. The Assembly was calling witnesses to examine NATO and, closer to Tom and Mark's concern, exactly how the Irish parliament came to decide on joining the organization and surrendering Ireland's traditional neutrality.

Tom told Mark that he was sure that Ambassador Pringle would block any efforts to get testimony from him and that both would protect Mark. The wild card, he confessed, was whether the American president might overrule his ambassador's decision.

Tom was sure that Foggy and his old boss, Mr. Jack Gobscheit, would be called to testify before the Assembly. Tom said he would give anything to listen in on that, but that he was understandably staying as far away from the Assembly as he could get and all its proceedings were closed to the public. In this regard, it was not dissimilar to an American grand jury.

CHAPTER

42

ONI Calls Again

Mark Jamison was half expecting the call. The head of the Office of Naval Intelligence was on the line, asking if he would consider another stint of active service to help keep Ireland in NATO.

"Captain, you made the right contacts in your year there and did remarkable service. This would be to help cement what you accomplished."

Jamison explained he would need to discuss the matter with his wife and would call back the following day. What he really wanted to tell her was: "No, hell no, and what nerve you have to even ask me. It would put me in peril as much as having Harrington send me off to Portmagee in one of the century's worst storms. Absolutely, unequivocally no!"

But Jamison learned to take his time with weighty decisions and the excuse of discussing the matter with Sarah was one that the admiral, also a wife and mother, could not easily dismiss. And so,

Mark did raise the matter of his going back to Dublin. Sarah said only that going back together with the kids for a family vacation was the only way either of them should consider it. They also agreed that it would be too soon to go back for at least another year.

"Then we are in full agreement that I stay put here at Angel Landing?"

"Yes, absolutely. Tell anyone who is pushing you that you did your duty and then some. I'm positive there are others out there willing to do whatever is required."

Mark welcomed Sarah's words, though his mind had already been made up.

Getting back to the admiral the next day was challenging, even with his mind made up. He thought the conversation resembled a dance of birds with one intent on mating, and the other fleeing for its life. The admiral was a very persuasive and determined individual. In the end, Mark had to mention his exposure to testifying under oath, even though he shouldn't have on an unsecure phone line, as well as domestic felicity. The latter held no weight.

Only time would tell, however, and no orders came. Mark felt secure to learn as much as possible from Tom Harrington about the unfolding drama behind closed doors in Dublin. Who could have guessed that the gentleman they rode to the hounds with only weeks before was now part of a pivotal group that would have great influence on the course of Ireland's policies. Mark recalled Seamus McGrath telling him that his career had been as a butcher in the local market. Would Seamus soon have the ability to question Jack Gobscheit? Maybe to determine whether Ireland stayed in NATO? It sure looked to Mark like democracy in action. Both Mark and Tom wished they could be in his shoes, or riding boots.

CHAPTER

43

The Ireland Citizens' Assembly

And so, it began. The Assembly convened with a great amount of background in Ireland's developing role and importance in Europe and the world. Mark suspected the inquiry would move from there to the Parliament and finally to a referendum on the future of Ireland in NATO. What would be uncovered along the way could only be guessed, but he didn't want anything pointing to him or Tom, and certainly not to Foggy, who was the sitting defense minister.

The Assembly began with Ireland's aim to be a "digital economy hot-spot in Europe" with data centers comprising a key part of this plan. As of April 2024, there were eighty-two data centers in Ireland, with an additional fourteen under construction, and planning approval granted for an additional forty centers.

Dublin's emergence as the largest data center cluster in Europe surpassed Frankfurt, London,

Amsterdam, and Paris. Ireland's strategic position in Northwestern Europe made it a key gateway to the continent, facilitated by its connection to the United States, Europe, and other regions through deep-sea fiber-optic cables.

Ireland's appeal was further enhanced by its highly educated workforce and its position as the only English-speaking nation within the European Union. Ireland's common law legal system formed a significant draw for foreign direct investment companies and its cool climate contributed to lower cooling costs for data centers. Furthermore, the Irish government had laid out a range of policy strategies to make Ireland an attractive destination for data centers and IT service providers, including supportive economic policies offering tax incentives.

Central to Ireland's growth in this vital sector was its submarine cables, which were critical infrastructure with no alternative. Satellite networks offer no comparison. The Assembly was told there were 574 active and planned submarine cables spanning nearly 1.4 million kilometers worldwide, carrying over 99 percent of all intercontinental communications using the latest in fiber-optic coherent optical transmission technology. The protection of this critical infrastructure was vital to Ireland, Europe, and the world.

Internet traffic was increasing at a 27 percent compound annual growth rate. The pandemic laid bare the need for connectivity with video conferences and livestreams to reach the outside world. Demand for reliable broadband only continued to increase. Ireland's future, the Assembly was informed, hinged upon the robust, high-speed core networks that subsea cable infrastructure provided.

In Ireland, just one provider, Meta, formerly known as Facebook, owned cables estimated to contribute $2.78 billion to the Irish economy each year. That impact was roughly equivalent to 15 percent of Ireland's typical GDP growth.

Adding resilience with another landing site, Meta and Microsoft teamed up with MAREA, the highest-capacity subsea cable to ever cross the Atlantic, connecting the data hub of Northern Virginia to Bilbao, Spain, and then to network hubs in Europe, Africa, the Middle East, and Asia. This route proceeded south of other transatlantic cable systems, thereby helping ensure more resilient and reliable connections for customers in the United States, Europe, and beyond. It boasted eight fiber pairs and an initial estimated design capacity of 160Tbps.

Another example of a content provider getting into the submarine cable business was Google, which had funded thirteen submarine cables in the last ten years.

Based on the ownership of the cables primarily by American-based multinationals, the Assembly next looked at whether NATO membership was essential to their protection. Wouldn't the companies that invested so heavily in them take on these measures? Furthermore, would NATO membership be a help or hindrance in negotiating with these companies? Members of the Assembly were expressing concern Brussels, not Dublin, could be in control of the very lifelines of Ireland's high-tech future. With the States backing some of its largest companies, and the outsized role of the USA in the affairs of NATO, wasn't Ireland risking its data center dominance in Europe? Finally, NATO's spending demands were looked at with great concern. Wouldn't they divert badly needed funds to major weapons purchases that couldn't be fulfilled domestically?

CHAPTER

44

Once a Hero

To examine how Ireland's parliament decided to join NATO, the current and former defense ministers were called by the Irish Citizens' Assembly to give testimony.

Defense Minister Gorgarty said they were still looking into the causes of the power outage that triggered parliament's vote, but they were assured and confident it was not the wrongdoing of any foreign power. As to the Russian fleet exercises at the time, permission had been given for both a Russian and NATO exercise. While he didn't agree with that decision at the time or since, the prior defense minister could shed more insight on his decision.

Gorgarty testified that Ireland was keeping up with its obligations to NATO and had a positive outlook on the relationship going forward. He said Ireland was more secure today as a result of membership and that defense industries were being created to fulfill its commitments to Brussels. Among those was a cable inspection and repair company without foreign participation. Subsea, the American-based NATO contractor, would continue serving in that role until a fully capable local company could be stood up. To the question about any threats to the cables, whether from a planted nuclear device or otherwise, he said unequivocally that Irish waters were secure and monitored regularly to ensure they would continue to be.

The defense minister also thanked NATO for its patience in allowing Ireland a grace period to get its defense spending up to the required 2 percent of GDP. He expressed confidence that the country's high-tech sector would continue to grow and thrive with the needs of NATO in the areas of systems security and the new priority they refer to as C4ISR. Foggy explained this stood for Command, Control, Communications, Computers, Intelligence, Surveillance, and Reconnaissance. He informed the Assembly that it was a military term referring to the network of systems and technologies used to collect, process, and disseminate information to support military operations.

The next witness was the most anticipated—the former defense minister, Jack Gobscheit. The Assembly members were keen to know about his time in Russia and what exactly went on during his discussions with Putin. Why was the public told that a nuclear device in its waters had been removed when it wasn't? And why did he approve a Russian naval exercise in their waters?

Gobscheit wanted to use the opportunity to regain some public standing from the relative obscurity in which he now found himself as deputy director of the office of fisheries management. Though faced with a hostile audience, none could say he failed to present his case persuasively.

Yes, he confessed, circumstances had changed when NATO canceled its naval exercise, but it was too late to call off that of the Russian Federation. Besides, monitoring of the cables showed nothing present after the exercises. Whatever the exercises did, they concluded with Irish waters safer than before.

With regard to Putin's promises at his dacha, Gobscheit remained convinced they were honestly made, but that implementing the decisions was the problem.

Gobscheit then proceeded to explain that his effort to keep Ireland safe and to preserve its neutrality remained the best course for Ireland. Getting Ireland locked into an arrangement where it surrendered its freedom of action would pull it into wars not of its choosing and curtail its humanitarian efforts. There were many levels of cooperation short of outright membership, as the nation had been pursuing for many years.

Jack continued by revealing his suspicions, based on years of following Britain's and America's propensity to incite hostilities. He claimed their governments stir up situations that support their weapons industries and advance the interests of their investment bankers around the world.

"London's financial center and Wall Street have no equivalent in Ireland, I'm pleased to say. But if we stay in NATO, we'll soon be needing to protect and grow the arms manufacturers they want us to develop. And that would be the good news from them. I can assure you that they are already knocking on Mr. Gorgarty's door trying to sell their own destructive products made in the US with invested British funds, sourced from around the world. We don't need to go there."

The Assembly asked him about the nation's own developing high-tech sector. Didn't it need the security offered by NATO?

"It has grown magnificently in an environment of our neutrality and independence. You heard earlier about C4ISR. I would rather have our sector grow systems to protect people, rather than commanding and controlling them. And surveilling them."

CHAPTER

45

Parliament Calls for a Referendum

The Assembly's recommendation to parliament was a resounding recommendation to opt out of NATO before its economy was turned into a vehicle for war production and involvement in conflicts not of its choosing around the world.

Parliament looked at the history of NATO, which had been an unquestionable success, but which had sustained "mission creep." It was no longer just a vehicle of mutual defense of its members, but was engaged around the world on other missions. It also suffered from a "group think" mentality, where conclusions of the leading members became policy adopted by all.

Parliament considered NATO's previous deployments in Bosnia and Herzegovina, Kosovo, Afghanistan, Iraq, and Libya and more recent pressures by the US for NATO to engage more actively with Indo-Pacific nations like Australia, Japan, South Korea, and New Zealand to counter what it viewed as threats posed by China. NATO's proclaimed platform to promote a rules-based international order and to defend democratic values and principles in the Indo-Pacific rang hollow in the Irish debates. Members of parliament raised how distant those values appeared when Irish relief assistance in the Middle East was being turned away and its UN peacekeepers were under assault with US-supplied weapons.

There was no think tank at NATO, at least of the sort that Jamison ran in Salzburg. Nor should there be really, he felt. The mission of NATO was actually very clear-cut, at least as far as it was intended to be. What it had turned into was another matter altogether.

Mark Jamison and Tom Harrington were delighted their names never came up either in the Assembly or parliamentary hearings. As Ireland prepared for a referendum, Brussels was frantic. No member had ever left the organization. What signal would it send? What would it bode for the remaining members, some of which would certainly like to follow in Ireland's wake, if it left?

Money mysteriously poured in for a campaign to keep the Emerald Isle safe and secure. Doubtless, enemies of NATO also weighed in.

Mark Jamison was delighted to be back in Angel Landing with no role in what was transpiring.

CHAPTER

46

Neutral Again

There was rejoicing across much of Ireland when the results of the referendum were confirmed. Ireland, the last country to join NATO, would be the first ever to leave it. The Irish president wrote to the US president to denounce membership and to notify the other members, which commenced the one-year waiting period for its separation and return to neutrality.

There was soon other news. Hungary's president announced it would also be leaving NATO. Now Mark Jamison really took a deep breath. The two countries he helped deliver to NATO were both pulling out of it.

He wasn't sure how to feel about his efforts ending like this. But as he looked at the results of his career, these were perhaps among the least troubling.

CHAPTER

47

Postscript

Many thought knocking out satellites in outer space would initiate the next global conflagration. As the thinking went, this would blind many sensors and could precede a nuclear attack. It was the reason the Americans created a new military branch of service: the Space Force.

Jamison was not convinced, however, that the old models applied any longer. In his thinking, the next war wouldn't call for a devastating nuclear attack at all. All that would be needed was unplugging the adversary from the source of its communications. In the case of NATO, this was a simple matter of cutting or jamming a few undersea cables.

So rather than the next war starting with a brazen attack on satellite systems, it could begin as easily as a coordinated dragging of heavy anchors along the seabed in key locations.

Ireland, as an island, would be particularly vulnerable. Its adding undersea electric energy cables to the mix, sharing power with the mainland, only added to the fragile dynamic at play.

Did Ireland belong in NATO after all? Was there another way to protect its connectivity?

Jamison looked back to international law and the gaping hole when it came to the oceans. The United States never even joined the Law of the Sea Convention, let alone facilitated protections for undersea cables. Was this because, as Edward Snowden disclosed, the NSA preferred the liberty of tapping into them from time to time?

Like so many others before him and many alongside him, Mark Jamison did his duty to help influence events. Although this adventure was over, he knew others would come along.

Sarah always kept a bag packed, after all.

ABOUT THE AUTHOR

Avery Mann is the pen name of Bruce Janigian, a retired naval captain, former diplomat, and think tank director who lived in a European castle, engaging some of the greatest minds of the planet. He remains connected to many secrets and loves to share the mystery of them in his novels.

THE MARK JAMISON ADVENTURES

Angel Landing: A Mark Jamison Thriller

Former government agent and think-tank director Mark Jamison needs a quiet coastal refuge for his breathing problems, and maybe some space to sort out his life and what remains of his marriage. What he finds in the mysterious little village of Angel Landing quickly escalates into a series of adventures to save the planet, or at least its male inhabitants, and soon forces him to confront his past and the assumptions that brought him here.

Persona Non Grata—End of the Great Game: A Mark Jamison Mystery

The Vatican and Kremlin are at the center of espionage and intrigue when they turn to Mark Jamison and a mysterious chess master to locate lost Byzantine treasures that could hold the key to world unity and peace. The end of the Cold War was only a resumption of the old Great Game, now more devastating than ever for the pawns on the chessboard of competing Middle East and Central Asian oil and gas pipelines. The answers go back further than the Silk Road, and the adventures to ferret them out span the old and new worlds, uncovering a forgotten past and lost knowledge at every turn. This thriller is as fast paced as it is historically accurate and prescient for what may well await us all.

Uncle Yeghia's Basement—What's Down There Is Not What You Suppose: A Mark Jamison Thriller

Charlie Epson pulls his oars against the tides every morning in a silent contest with his past. He is among a very special cohort monitored within the Angel Landing Yacht Club; those whose career misadventures in public service exposed them to matters never to be shared. Yes, this group needs to drink a lot, but like their glasses filled to the brim, they are permitted good conversation without spilling. When an old colleague winds up in the bay with a broken neck and former Soviet assassins arrive looking for laundered Ukrainian funds to help their war effort, Bjorn Ingman and Mark Jamison are once again called into action in this thrilling new mystery.

The Mark Jamison Adventures: A Trilogy

Many enjoyable intrigues in this series are factually based, offering insights into a world of deception and buried truths. What lies at the center of so many lies and so much conflict in today's world? After investigations around the world over many years, Jamison may have uncovered the key. "If you look deeply enough behind it all, you will find the hand of British Petroleum." But see for yourself, take the magical journey, travel the world, and climb down into the basement where pieces of the truth may be uncovered, buried under the debris of lies.

Printed in Great Britain
by Amazon